JAWS OF LIFE

JAWS OF LIFE

STORIES

LAURA LEIGH MORRIS

VANDALIA PRESS • MORGANTOWN 2018

ISBN:
Paper 978-1-946684-15-8
EPUB 978-1-946684-16-5
PDF 978-1-946684-17-2

Library of Congress Cataloging-in-Publication Data is
available from the Library of Congress

Book and cover design by Than Saffel / WVU Press

Stories in this collection previously appeared in the following publications:
"Frackers." *Bayou Magazine*, forthcoming
"Muddin'." *Appalachian Heritage*, Volume 44, Issue 3, Summer 2016
"May Ours Be as Happy as Yours." *Notre Dame Review*, Number 42, Summer/Fall 2016
"Grief." *Stoneboat Literary Journal*, 6.2, Spring 2016
"Jaws of Life." *The Louisville Review*, Volume 77, Spring 2015
"The Dance." *Tulane Review*, Spring 2015
"Controlled Fall." *Conclave: A Journal of Character*, Issue 8, Fall 2014
"The Dollar General." *Weave Magazine*, Issue 11, Summer 2014
"A Room with a Door." *Qwerty Magazine*, Spring 2014
"The Tattoo." *Tattoos*. Ed. Alice Osborn. Charlotte, NC:
Mainstreet Rag Publishing Co., 2012

For my parents,
Ron and Sue Morris,
who have always believed in me

CONTENTS

———

ACKNOWLEDGMENTS

———

For all the people who have been there over years of drafting, revising, editing, and complaining. In no particular order: Angie Cruz, Catalina Bartlett, Amber Foster, Ryan Neighbors, and David Levinson, who were there from the very beginning; Magda Bogin, who helped turn those early drafts into something worthwhile; Ron and Sue Morris, my parents to whom this book is dedicated, who cheer me on with every step forward; Alma Villanueva, who has been a writing buddy and a true friend through this process; Laith Alsaab, who was always there for a hug when the day felt long; Colleen Thorndike, who was there for the long haul; David Gross, who listened as I read the entire manuscript out loud and has cheered me on throughout the revision and publishing process; the magazines that believed in the work enough to publish individual stories; Furman University for the financial support that helped me to finish it and find a publisher; Abby Freeland, my editor at Vandalia, who has put up with all of the questions from this first time author; Joni Tevis, who has been a mentor/friend extraordinaire; the women of Bryan Federal Prison Camp, who listened to me talk about writing every day; Larry Heinemann, who helped me think through what I'm trying to do in these stories; the people of West Virginia who live their lives and are the inspiration for all the stories in this collection; all of those I forgot to mention but were there for the creation of this book. Thank you, all.

FRACKERS

——

Picture it: four industrial bulbs, 1,000+ watts each, trained on the house all night. And it doesn't matter if I use blackout curtains or move to another room—there's no way to ignore the production happening just a quarter mile from my bedroom window. I can hear the workers yelling, the whine of machinery, the wrecks that sometimes happen because drivers are confused by the brightness. I can see the lights through closed eyelids.

When you're looking at a check full of zeroes for just a few acres of land, you think about a new roof, replacing the furnace that hasn't kept the house properly warm in at least ten years. You think about how you won't have to pinch pennies until the beginning of the next month. You don't think about the fact that fracking is a twenty-four-hour business. Or that they'll point their lights straight at your bedroom window, then claim it's the only angle that works.

For six months, I called Jameson Wells, the county, the state, anyone I could get on the phone. Everywhere I turned, I received the same stony silence. So I got out of bed one night at midnight and slid off my nightgown, replacing it with black pants and shirt, black shoes, my white hair tied up under a black hat. They wouldn't see me coming.

I crouched behind trees and crawled across the field on my elbows, a serious undertaking for a woman my age. About fifty yards off, I lay on the ground and caught my breath. Then, I pulled the BB gun off my back and aimed for center mass. There was a small ping and then a tinkle of broken glass as the first bulb burst. The men hadn't figured out what was going on before I'd shattered two more. I never got a chance with the final bulb. They'd realized what was happening and turned the light from my line of sight. As their voices filled the night air, I crawled back to my house and slid into my bed without anyone realizing I'd been gone. It was the soundest I'd slept in months.

* * *

"Did you see anything?" everyone wanted to know at the Pantry Store the next morning. Word had traveled fast. I'd barely poured my coffee when the old-timers crowded around me. For at least twenty years, we'd all woken before the sun and made our way to the convenience store in the middle of town to sip coffee and trade stories before anyone else even thought about starting their day. Miller James, the night guy, always had a fresh pot of coffee brewing by 5 a.m., and I usually poured the first cup. Today, I was twenty minutes late, and the others had already drunk a full pot and taken most of the chairs.

"See any what?" I asked.

"The lights, Mabel," Dewey said. His grin stretched across his face, his eyes crinkling at the corners. He looked like someone had announced an extra month of buck season. "Someone shot the lights out."

"Really?" I asked. "That must be why I overslept."

They all laughed. I'd been complaining about the lights since the drilling began, showing up at the Pantry Store sometimes as early as 3 a.m., bags under my eyes, drinking cup after cup of coffee to stay alert.

As soon as everyone was quiet, Dewey leaned forward, his elbows on the table. "You know what this means?" he asked. Everyone turned to him. "Someone's finally standing up for us."

They all started talking at once. A few hit the table with their fists for emphasis.

Dewey always said Jameson Wells didn't care about Brickton, just about its profits. In fact, when I sold that land to them, he didn't speak to me for two weeks. Kept referring to me as "that traitor" whenever he could. When he got over that, we settled on not talking about Jameson or my land. When I said something about the lights, he said I may as well move closer to town, buy myself a condo. Then, I didn't speak to him for a week. My grandparents had built my house, and my family had owned that land as far back as I could figure. I might have given up some of it, but I'd be damned if I was going to move into a cardboard condo.

I leaned back in my chair, crossed my arms over my chest, and watched them yell at each other. I couldn't hear a word, but Dewey waved his finger in Dan Morgan's face. Harold Travers half stood from his chair and stared down Sutter Smith, who looked like he might throw a left hook at any second.

"Hey," Miller yelled from behind the counter. No one paid him any mind. He made his way over to our table, put two fingers in his mouth, and let out a piercing whistle. Everyone stopped. "Y'all take it outside if you want to fight," he said. "This is a business."

I sipped my coffee. Dewey dropped his finger, Harold sat down, and the high color drained from Sutter's face. Miller huffed loudly and went back behind the counter. Usually, we were a quiet crowd, retired people looking to shoot the shit and drink some coffee. Unless the coal mines or fracking came up. Then, well—then we got told where to go.

"They're saying they were ambushed," Dewey added. Quietly now.

Everyone nodded. No one spoke for a minute. When we'd first heard that Jameson Wells was coming to Brickton, we thought every-one would have a job and we'd all be rich. Turns out, those of us who owned land with gas deposits under it did get a nice lump of cash, but there weren't many jobs for people in town. Instead, the company imported workers from Texas and Oklahoma, people who'd spent their whole lives drilling for oil and gas. The only people who made any money were those who had an extra room to rent, and they could and did charge anything they wanted for a place to sleep. Everyone else in town was still waiting for the coal mines to call back workers from the most recent round of layoffs. Or for Jameson to hire on locals at the wells. We'd all heard the gas deposit was bigger and deeper than anyone had thought. That soon enough, there'd be jobs for anyone who wanted. We were still waiting on that. We also heard that soon enough those of us who had houses over the deposits would be forced out completely, but I wasn't going anywhere.

"Well, whoever did it is my hero," I said. I wrapped my hands around my mug of coffee to keep the chill off. Wearing work boots and a quilted flannel over my sweater, I still couldn't get warm. Summer had slipped away, and I wasn't used to the cold morning air. "I don't give a damn about the politics, but I haven't slept like that in who knows how long."

"You should care about the politics," Dewey said. He was quieter this time, gentler when he talked to me. He'd had a thing for me ever since my husband, Irwin, died ten years earlier. Sometimes, I cooked a rhubarb pie and brought it by his house. We ate it with cups of milk before moving to the back porch to smoke cigars and sip a nice scotch, but it didn't go any further than that. After so much time alone, I think we were both too nervous. Or too damn tired. Maybe that was as far as we'd ever go.

We weren't much interested in more. What we wanted was to sit down next to someone who had air rushing in and out of their lungs, blood pumping through their veins. In my whole life, I'd never been on my own—I'd moved from my parents' house to Irwin's. And when he'd died, a few years after Dewey's wife died, we two old-timers were on our own. And so far, at least, we were doing the best we could to keep each other company.

"The cops'll figure it out," I said, and everyone laughed. Our police were mostly kids not far out of high school who would give you a ticket for going twenty-eight in a twenty-five but didn't know a damn thing about detective work.

"I'll stop by this evening," Dewey said. "We can sit on your porch and enjoy the night air."

"That'd be good," I said. "Real good." It had been a long time since I'd enjoyed an evening at home—too much light. But without the Jameson people, the sunset on the hills behind my house was the prettiest you'd find in all of Marion County.

Conversations split off, each person offering a theory on who'd shot out the lights. Never once did my name come up. After all, I was sixty-eight years old, and I was the one who'd sold the land to that damn company to begin with. Dewey put his hand over mine, and we listened to the yarns spin around us.

* * *

"Don't bother coming out," I said to Dewey over the phone that evening.

Just as the shadows had started to creep into crevices between the hills, a van had pulled up with five new lights. Even though it wasn't anywhere near dark, the workers pointed them in my direction and turned them on.

I sat on my porch all evening facing them. When I shaded my eyes, I could see they had more men on site than usual, and a lot of them were milling around, keeping an eye on the hills surrounding them, looking for saboteurs, no doubt. I watched them swivel from side to side, an eye on everything, and I sipped at two fingers of scotch. Eventually, I got hungry and walked inside, where the air was warm and light filtered through everything. I had blackout curtains up everywhere, but beams of light still shot through around the edges. Even if the curtains worked better, it wouldn't matter. Light shone through the gaps in the door and window frames.

The darkness was too good to last, and I knew it. Besides, they may as well have been pumping cold, hard cash out of the ground over there. No way they were going to let the well stay idle for a minute longer than they had to.

Suddenly, there was a loud crash, and the lights dimmed. People were yelling. I opened my door, stepped back on the porch, and saw headlights pointed at an odd angle, up toward the trees. They came from a truck sitting in the middle of the site, having run through a fence, across half the work area, and over some equipment, stopping only feet from the main well. It looked like it was hung up on a whole pile of things it had run through, tilted a bit to the side. Someone had already pointed the industrial lights at the wreck, so I had a good view of men standing around the truck, some scratching their heads, others yelling at the driver. I squinted but couldn't see him well. I recognized the truck though, a dull yellow Ford F-250 that belonged to Harold Travers.

I sat on the porch swing, all my breath gone. The whole thing looked like the type of accident I'd been warning people about for months—someone not familiar with the road gets blinded by the lights, confused by the odd bends in the road, and runs right over the hill and into the site. I was surprised it hadn't happened before now.

Except Harold wasn't some newcomer to these roads. He lived two miles farther out and drove past the site daily, had lived in the same place his whole life and could drive these roads with his eyes closed. Hell, his truck probably knew where it was going without Harold pointing it in the right direction.

I sat on that swing for hours, ignoring the hunger in my gut and the four times my phone rang. The police showed up, then paramedics who shone lights in Harold's eyes. Eventually, a tow truck arrived and pulled his truck off the heap of debris. Official vehicles arrived. More people looked at the damage. More people yelled.

Still, the sounds of the site were muted, work put on hold while they took care of the accident. The lights weren't even pointed at my house. It was dark enough that if I just went inside, I could sleep like a baby. But I didn't. I sat on my porch swing, my hands limp in my lap, and watched everything.

* * *

"We old guys get confused sometimes," Harold said. He tried to keep the grin off his face but failed. "Those lights, man, they blinded me. Just like Mabel said." He winked at me. "It was just a matter of time before someone got confused and ran straight through that fence."

I ignored him and moved to the stand of coffee pots. I grabbed one to refill my cup but realized it was still full. The guys at the table guffawed at Harold. I stared at my coffee, unable to return to them. On my way into town this morning, I'd noticed more than just his wreck. The official sign to the site was now covered in graffiti. Handmade signs stood on either side of the road denouncing Jameson Wells. There were at least a hundred of them, from the site itself all the way into town. The brick exterior of the Pantry Store was spray-painted with an X over the word *fracking*. Jameson trucks sporting slashed tires sat in a lot across the street.

Had I caused this? I hadn't meant to. I'd just wanted a little peace and quiet. A full night's sleep. Harold continued to regale them with the details of his crash, shaking his head over the damage he'd done. "It's a shame," he said. "No clue how long that well will be down."

"At least you'll be able to sleep," Dewey whispered in my ear, and

I jumped, dropping my mug on the counter. It didn't shatter, but a deep crack formed up the side, and coffee began to seep across the formica.

"Shit," I said and grabbed a handful of paper towels. My cheeks burned as I blotted the mess.

Dewey put his hands over mine, stopping them. "Mabel?" he said.

I shook my head, pulled my hands from his, and dropped the broken mug in the trash. I wiped up the rest of the spilled coffee. Dewey didn't move, didn't speak either.

Finally, I said, "I shot out the lightbulbs." Whispered it really.

"What?"

I said it again, louder, and met his eye. He looked away, then back at me, mouth half open. Then, he began to laugh, one of those laughs that erupts straight from your belly and rocks your whole frame.

Harold fell quiet, and the guys looked over at us. What a sight we were too, me standing there meek and red-faced, Dewey towering over me, laughing so hard tears ran down his cheeks.

"Never mind," I said. I threw the rest of the paper towels in the trash and walked toward the exit.

"Mabel," Dewey called after me, but I kept going.

* * *

The Jameson Wells people were impressive, really. I sat on my porch all day and into the evening. As the sun started to set, they put up even more lights. Some shone toward my house, others toward the woods that surrounded them, even more toward the damage they were repairing at record speed.

"You started something," Dewey said, and I jumped.

The noise from the well was too loud to hear him come up the driveway, and I was too taken by the work to notice him walk around my house. He stood at the foot of my stairs, one boot propped on the bottom step.

"Don't you dare come up here," I said. He was breaking a rule. Whenever we fought over Jameson, we each took to our own spaces, cooling off before we tried to talk. The phone had been ringing all day, and since he was the only one who ever called, I hadn't answered. I sipped from a glass of scotch and watched the frackers at work.

"You started something," Dewey said again, but he removed his foot from my step and put his hands in his pockets. "Whether you meant to or not."

"Of course I didn't," I said. I didn't look at him.

"You can't stop it," he said.

"I don't see why you give a shit," I said. Dewey was seventy-three, long retired from the coal mines, with a nice pension and Social Security. If fracking really was as bad as they said, Dewey would be long dead by the time anything happened. I opened my mouth to say so but then closed it. We'd had this conversation before. More than once. That's why we didn't talk when we were mad. He was too damn stubborn to listen. So was I. We worked better if we shut up about some things.

Dewey turned his back to me and watched the Jameson people clean up the site. We sat like that until the sun was clear over the hills, only the spotlights illuminating the night. I went inside, added another couple fingers of scotch to my glass. I thought about getting one for Dewey, decided not to, then relented. It was cold out, and a stiff drink would keep the shivers at bay. I pushed the screen door open with my back and came onto the porch. The door slapped against the metal frame. I opened my mouth to invite Dewey up for one drink, but he was gone. I thought about sitting out there and drinking them both, but it was cold, and the lights hurt my eyes. I went back inside.

* * *

It had been six nights since Harold drove through the fence, five since Dewey and I had spoken, and the lights were brighter than ever. They'd fixed the site, and the well was working at full force again, but they'd kept all the extra lights. Beams shot across my bedroom. The whine of machinery filled my head. I stared up at the ceiling and watched the shapes change as the lights moved. When I did drift off for a few minutes, fracking filled my dreams. Sleeping, waking, I couldn't tell the difference.

I'd been going to the Pantry Store, sitting in my usual chair beside him, but on the fifth day, when Dewey said, "You can't keep going on like this," I held my hand up.

"Not yet," I said. "I'm not ready."

"You're the one who sold the land," he said.

I looked at him for the first time in days. "I can't," I said. "Really, I can't do this." I was desperate. I would scream if he said one more word. I was sleeping less than ever, drinking more and more coffee every morning, but my thoughts were getting fuzzier. I couldn't make sense of him or anything else. I wasn't ever fully asleep or awake. Those damn lights filled my mind until they were all I could think about.

He looked at me for a minute, must have seen something, because he nodded. He reached out, grabbed my fingers. I let him.

By the time I got out of bed, it was midnight, my eyes burned, and all I could think about was those damn lights. They haunted me. I put on the same black clothes from the week before and even covered my face with shoe polish I found in the pantry. By the time I walked out the back door, I blended perfectly with what darkness there was.

Instead of crouching for some of the trek across the field, I stayed on my stomach the whole way, pulling myself along with my elbows until I made it to the tall grass near where they worked, away from the trees. All week, men had patrolled the site, looking toward the woods for a saboteur, which made sense, as they offered the most cover, but I was smarter than them. I was right in thinking they wouldn't pay much attention to a tall stand of grass.

Once there, I stopped to catch my breath and rest a minute before commencing with my plan. I'd crawled the length of almost four football fields, and I could feel it in my whole body. Last week, I was sore. Tonight, I'd go home covered in bruises. Sweat beaded on my face, and my breath was too ragged to take a good shot. Besides, even if I hit the lights, I still had to get back to my house without getting caught.

"Break," I heard a man call and lifted my head. I watched as half the men milling around made their way to a trailer on the edge of the work site. As they walked through the door, I noticed that most of them carried guns across their backs. My breath caught in my throat. I hadn't noticed that before. All I had was a BB gun—it wouldn't create more than a welt on a person's skin.

I realized I wouldn't have a better chance than now. I aimed at the light farthest from me and heard a ping, metal on metal, but the light still shone. "Dammit," I muttered and aimed again. None of the men had noticed what I was doing yet. I breathed deep and then let my breath out. At the moment my lungs were empty, I squeezed the trigger and watched as the light went dark.

"Hey," one of the men yelled, and then there was a jumble of sounds as they gathered around that light, each looking in a different direction, many pulling guns to their shoulders and searching through their scopes. These men had hunted before, were good shots, used to killing dinner for their families.

While they were still confused, not quite sure where to look, I aimed at a second light and took it out too. "Over there!" a man yelled, and I looked to see him pointing in my direction. No clue how he'd seen me in the darkness, no muzzle flash on a BB gun, but he'd spotted me just the same.

I didn't wait for them to come my way. I stood, hoped wearing full body black would hide me long enough to get away from them, at least far enough that no one could get a good shot off. I even ran in zigzags, like I'd seen people do in movies, hoping they wouldn't be able to keep me in their sights long enough.

I was almost far enough away that they wouldn't be able to get a good bead on me when I heard the crack of a shotgun, and my shoulder felt like it was on fire as buckshot buried itself in the meat of my flesh. I cried out, almost fell, but I didn't. I dropped the BB gun, useless to me now, and ducked low as I ran toward my house.

Even in that much pain, I wasn't stupid enough to climb the steps to my porch. Instead, I ran around my house and down the stairs into the basement. There, I made my way upstairs and into my kitchen. I dropped into a chair at the table and let myself feel the full force of the buckshot in my shoulder.

I laid my head on the table and maybe blacked out for a second, then let myself cry a few tears before pulling it together. I reached for the phone and paused. I couldn't call 911, couldn't go to the hospital. I took a deep breath and dialed Dewey.

"You have to come over right now," I said.

"What's going on?" he asked, sleep in his voice. It was the middle of the night.

"Now," I said.

There was silence. Then, "I'll be right there."

I hung up and laid my forehead on the table. I practiced breathing evenly. Blood ran down my arm, pooled in my lap, but I didn't look at my shoulder. I wiggled my toes, the fingers on my good hand, and paid attention to staying conscious until Dewey arrived.

I heard the front door open, called, "In here."

When he caught sight of me, Dewey was in the middle of unzipping his coat. He stopped, his hand still gripping the zipper tab. His eyes got bigger, his mouth opened. No sound came out. I tried to smile but didn't quite pull it off.

"What the hell happened?" he asked once he'd found his voice.

"I got shot," I said.

"Oh, God," he said, his voice weak. He rushed toward me, started to lift me, said, "We need to get you to a hospital."

"No," I said. "No hospital."

He lowered me back in the chair. Pain shot through my shoulder, and I breathed through my teeth until it passed. Dewey's hands hovered over me, as though wanting to help but afraid to hurt.

"What can I do?" he asked.

"Fix it," I said.

"I can't." He backed away, his hands up.

"You have to."

He dropped his hands, which were now shaking visibly. "Shit," he muttered. He paced to across the floor, back. "Shit," he said again. He turned from me, walked toward the living room, but stopped in the doorway. He gripped the door jam with both hands, took a deep breath, then turned back to me. "Okay," he said. Then again," Okay," as though steeling himself.

He left the room, and I heard him searching my linen closet, tossing things he didn't need onto the floor. He returned with a pile of towels and every bandage I owned, along with a prescription bottle. He popped the lid and handed me two pills. "What is it?" I asked.

"This is going to hurt like hell," he said. "You don't want to feel it."

I put the pills in my mouth and dry swallowed.

"Let's see what you did to yourself," he said and took a pair of scissors to my jacket. He cut quickly and then pulled the cloth from my skin more slowly. Where the blood had already started to clot, the shirt had dried to my skin. When he tried to pull it, I cried out, was already glad for the pills, and hoped they started working soon. Dewey soaked the fabric in water until it was soft enough to remove. Slowly, he took the clothes from my upper body and washed away some of the blood. Water tinged pink splashed the linoleum floor.

"It could be worse," he said.

"How?" I asked. The words were getting harder to form.

"If you'd been closer, I'd have to take you to the hospital." He pressed his fingers into my back, and I yelped, though the pain felt muted, almost like it was happening to someone else. "It's not too deep. And there's only a handful of buckshot in your shoulder. I think I can get it out."

It didn't feel like a handful, and he didn't sound sure. "Let me see," I said.

"You sure?"

"Yeah," I said. "Grab the hand mirrors in the bathroom."

He returned with two and laid one beside my head. I forced myself up on my good arm. "Easy," he said. "You'll make it start bleeding again." He held up the other mirror, and I could see the holes in my back, just a few of them. They looked tiny, too small to cause so much pain and blood. My face looked silly now, smeared in shoe polish.

"I need to dig out the buckshot," Dewey said. He was pale, his lips the same color as his skin. "Even with the pills, it'll hurt. Bad."

I nodded and handed him the mirror. I laid my face on the table again. "There's rubbing alcohol in the pantry and tweezers in my makeup bag."

While he was gone, there was a knock on the door. "Who're you?" I heard the man ask.

"Dewey Trotts."

"Where's the lady who lives here?"

"She's sick," Dewey said. "In bed."

"Did either of you see what happened out here?" the man asked.

Dewey said something I couldn't hear.

But the man replied loud and clear, explaining that someone had shot out their lights.

"We've been inside all night," Dewey said. "Haven't seen a thing."

"You mind if I come in?"

"Hey, hey, hey," Dewey said. He sounded angry. "What the hell do you think you're doing?" I could picture him, shoving that guy backward, out of my doorway. "You got no one's permission to come in here. It's the middle of the night. You want to see her, you come back in the daytime and ask Mabel nicely if you can visit." The door slammed, and I felt Dewey's footsteps as he stomped back to the kitchen.

"What the hell did you think you were doing?" he asked, angry now.

"I couldn't sleep," I said. "Besides, what Harold did was worse."

"You sold them the land," he said. He slapped the table beside my head. I cringed.

"I didn't know they'd make my life hell," I said.

"I told you they would."

He had. He said not to trust them, but I'd never believed him. Not really.

"You said I started something," I said.

"You did." He poured rubbing alcohol on the tweezers. "But I think it's time to stop it." I looked up at him. He looked tired. Sad.

"You said I couldn't."

"Then maybe it's time to step away from it. You're not safe."

At that moment, the lights came on again, their beams cutting across my yard, through the windows, and into Dewey's eyes. Sweat shone on his face.

"I don't think I can step away," I said. "Not now."

He was silent, staring into the lights. Then, slowly, "You're right in the middle of it."

"I am," I said.

"You know, I have a .30-30," he said.

"That changes the whole game," I said.

"They changed the game first," he said, "when they started shooting old ladies."

"I still have Irwin's .30-06."

"You're out of this now."

I shook my head, cringed at even that small movement. The painkillers weren't dulling the pain enough. I thought about asking for another but didn't. I needed to feel the pain.

"You're out of this," he repeated.

"Not if you take out the buckshot and bandage me up."

"I'll do that," he said. "But you're still out."

"I'm in the middle of it," I said.

He looked at the lights and then back at me, still sprawled half naked across my table, my shoulder covered in tiny holes. He didn't answer. Instead, he pulled his chair close to mine and began to probe at the wounds with the tweezers. I bit my lip at the pain but didn't cry out. My tears pooled on the table, but Dewey didn't react. He worked with clinical precision, probing each of the holes, digging the tweezers into my flesh, and removing the buckshot one at a time.

Once, I said, "Dewey," but he said, "I can't." Real quiet. A whisper. I didn't ask him what he couldn't do. Instead, I breathed slowly, fought the desire to scream, and watched as he placed each piece of buckshot on the table, a little line of steel balls so close to my face I could barely see them.

BRICKTON BOYS

—

Brandon stood in the parking lot an hour after the Brickton Bobcats won the football game because his dad told him to make nice with the boss's kids. He was cold and wet, his shoes soaked through and covered in mud. Ernie and Oscar Imogen stood in front of him, both with their chests puffed out, their Carhartt jackets still creased from the packaging, the rim of snuff cans in their back pockets barely showing through the Levis that may as well have had the price tags on them. Their costumes would be funny if the two weren't bearded manlings who looked like they'd be more at home in the mines than in a high school classroom.

Ernie and Oscar Imogen had showed up in Brickton at the beginning of the school year from Massachusetts. They'd arrived in camouflage, work boots, flannel shirts buttoned to their chins, looking every bit the mountain man that West Virginia was supposed to produce. Except they were born in Jersey, had spent their childhoods in DC, Brickton their tenth home in as many years, according to Brandon's dad. And if you looked closely, their work boots had never been used for work. Their flannels still held the shape of the store hanger, their camouflage had never seen the woods. The first person to laugh at their faux mountain-man costumes was Tim Schwarz, and he'd walked away from that encounter with a couple broken ribs, unwilling to name Ernie or Oscar as the offender. Without proof, they'd been spared a three-day suspension and gained a reputation, along with whispers of past violence at their previous schools. Now, everyone gave them a wide berth, no one chancing eye contact in case their ribs would be the next to break.

So, when Brandon's dad told him the brothers were having trouble making friends, it was his job to ride with them to the football game and make sure they had a good time. Of course, when they'd arrived in a brand-new Ford F-150 to pick him up, they'd *yessir-ed* his dad, but after they left the house, they were pure swagger. From the moment they'd arrived at the game, they'd been itching for a fight, purposely shoulder-checking kids from class, forcing people to slide down the bleachers to make room for them to spread their legs. No one had taken the bait. Until now.

Ernie and Oscar stood too close to a boy with an acne-scarred face. Brandon stepped to the side, not willing to get involved. "I don't think you know where you are," Ernie was saying to the boy. His cheeks were etched with lines Brandon thought you could only get in your forties, the kind you get from years of sun and hard work. He wondered if Ernie had been held back. He was a senior but looked well over twenty. Maybe thirty.

"I didn't mean to cause any trouble," the boy said, already backing toward his beat-up Toyota Corolla. Brandon wasn't sure what the boy had done, wasn't sure he'd done anything, wasn't sure that mattered to Ernie and Oscar. He didn't recognize the kid either—probably someone from Fallwell who didn't know the Imogens' reputation.

"This is Brickton," Oscar said and stepped even closer to the boy. Oscar was younger than Ernie, only a sophomore, but he sported a full beard. "You made trouble by coming here."

Ernie stepped forward too, his chest pressed to the boy's, but Brandon hung back. His dad had told him to make nice with the

Imogens, make them feel at home, but he hadn't signed up for a fight. The Toyota driver and his friends didn't say anything, though the color drained from their faces. Oscar took another step forward. "You don't belong here," he said. Neither do you, Brandon thought, but kept quiet.

Oscar was no bigger than the driver of the Toyota, maybe a couple inches shorter even, but he'd win if it came to blows. Where the other boy cowered, Oscar and Ernie never wavered. A few onlookers were gathered around them, parents and friends of the football team, waiting for the end of postgame meetings. Brandon recognized some of them, people he went to school with, parents of his friends. He shrunk back, keeping as much space as possible between himself and the Imogens.

"You should leave now," Ernie said.

Toyota boy and his friends turned and ran. They barely had the doors to the car closed when the driver spun out of the muddy lot.

Brandon breathed a sigh of relief, even as Ernie yelled, "Pussies!" after the car.

"Ready to go?" Brandon asked.

Both brothers turned to look at him. "Got somewhere to be?" Oscar asked, a bit of New England slipping into his faux Southern accent.

Brandon looked away, watched as parents and teens wandered off now that they realized there wouldn't be a fight. A few people whispered and glanced back at them, including Marsha Vance, who was in his homeroom for the second year in a row and who he'd been thinking of asking to homecoming. He nixed that idea.

At school, everyone steered clear of the Imogens, but behind their backs, people laughed, aping their mountain man posturing. Just being seen with them had lowered Brandon's cool factor, but he remembered his dad's words: "You have to get along with these guys, make nice. You do this for me, and I'll owe you. Anything you want." He'd seemed almost embarrassed as he said it. After a moment he added, "It's on you," and averted his gaze.

Ernie and Oscar's dad had been brought in to streamline things at one of the Jameson Wells, to see where they could cut corners and add to public opinion after the local fracking industry had suffered from some bad publicity. Brandon's dad had only been brought on to appease the people who said Jameson didn't hire any locals. Now that they were looking to cut where they could, getting rid of a guy who didn't have any experience was the obvious place to start.

Brandon's dad had spent the last few years in and out of work, being laid off and called back to the mines repeatedly. Some months, he could afford their bills and had a few dollars left over. Other months, they stopped by the Food Pantry for boxes of canned goods. So, when Mr. Imogen said, "Isn't your boy the same age as my youngest?" his dad had said, "Yes, sir, he is." That was when their family's livelihood fell on Brandon's shoulders, and right now he felt the full weight of it.

"Want to grab some burgers?" he asked them.

"What are you, chicken shit?" Oscar asked. He crowded Brandon, who stepped back, but Ernie wasn't paying attention, so Oscar backed off. He seemed to act only under Ernie's command, fading into the background the rest of the time, rubbing his beard and flexing beefy muscles that he was ready to use if ordered.

"I'm gonna teach those pussies a lesson," Ernie said, staring toward the road.

"They didn't do anything," Brandon said.

Ernie ignored him. Oscar turned to Brandon. "You can find a ride home with one of the mommies and daddies over there. Wouldn't want you to get your panties in a bunch."

Ernie snickered, and Brandon felt his face turn red. Ernie turned to Oscar and said, "Let's go."

Oscar jumped in the back of the truck, and Brandon scrambled to catch up. He had to grab the lip of the bed to climb the jacked up frame, and he almost fell when his Nike slipped off the bumper, but he threw himself into the bed just as Ernie hit the gas. His sweatshirt wasn't warm enough in the wind whipping past them as Ernie sped out of the school gates and took a right toward Brickton proper.

Brandon looked up to where Oscar sat on the giant toolbox that was bolted below the truck's cab. He was holding out a bottle of Bud and sipping on another. Brandon scooted over to the box, hoisted himself up, and took a long swallow of beer. It tasted awful, but he continued to sip and tried to remain perched on the toolbox as the truck bounced down side roads in search of the Toyota. Ernie pulled open the window in the back of the cab and said, "Gimme one." Oscar passed him a bottle, and Brandon held his cold hands toward the cab's heated air. Then, Ernie yelped. At first, Brandon thought it was over the beer before realizing he'd spotted the Toyota, which was driving slowly in front of them. Oscar called out too. Then, Ernie sped to catch up.

They whooped and hollered when the truck's bumper tapped the back of the car they were chasing. The Toyota fishtailed, and Ernie braked and gave the little car room to recover before riding its ass. Oscar cheered and urged Ernie to hit the car again, but Brandon stayed quiet. He watched in horror as Oscar drained the last of his beer and then lobbed the empty bottle at the car. It smashed against the back window, and he grabbed other empties that rolled around the bed of the truck and began throwing those at the Toyota too. Some hit, and a small crack formed on the back window. The wind caught the others and sent them flying backward.

"What's your problem, asshole?" Brandon looked up to see Oscar staring him down. He shook his head and looked away, but Oscar shoved him and said, "I'm talking to you."

Brandon almost fell off the toolbox but grabbed the edge to steady himself. "Me?" he said.

"You see any other assholes here?"

Brandon remembered his dad's face, his averted eyes, the color high in his cheeks, the way every word seemed hard for him to utter. He remembered his dad's directive to "make nice." He looked at the bottle he'd been sipping from. He gripped the neck, stood, and hurled it at the car. It burst against the back window, beer and bits of glass everywhere. The crack in the window spider webbed outward. "No assholes here," he said.

Oscar stared at him, and Brandon forced himself not to look away even though his heart was beating too fast and he could feel sweat running down his sides. He held onto the spotlights on top of the truck's cab to keep his balance as Ernie swerved. Oscar didn't even do that—he stood in a wide stance, perfectly balanced in the unsteady truck. Then, he smiled and slapped Brandon on the back. "Not bad, little man," he said. "Not too bad." Ernie whooped out the back window, and Brandon forced himself to join in.

Then, the ball of fear that had first lodged itself in his stomach when he'd almost slipped from the bumper grew. "You scared him," Brandon called through truck's rear window. "Isn't that enough?"

"Hell, no," Ernie said and sped up again. "Don't be a pussy." This time, they hit the car harder, and one of its taillights shattered.

Brandon sat on the giant toolbox and held on tight. Oscar continued to stand, one hand now gripping the spotlights as he whooped. Then, he leaned down and grabbed Brandon's shoulder. "Listen, kid," he said. "They could have gone home. Then, none of this would have happened. It's their fault."

"They were here for the football game," Brandon said. "Just like us."

"That's not the point," Oscar said. "They had a choice. When they left the field, they could have driven home. But look where we are—in Brickton. They're the ones who decided they weren't leaving."

Brandon nodded, but his heart sank. If the boys in the Toyota had turned left when they exited the lot, they'd have been on their way home. Instead, they had turned right, toward Brickton. Of course,

Brandon doubted they could have changed anything. Ernie and Oscar would have found a different reason to wreak havoc.

The little car sped up, and its motor whined louder. Brandon wanted to tell the people in it to slow down, to be careful. He wasn't sure what Ernie would do to them if their car's motor blew. The Toyota slid in gravel and pinged off the guardrail as it took a quick left, but it didn't stop. The truck followed, but Ernie slowed a bit for the turn, and the Toyota gained ground. Brandon breathed a sigh of relief.

"Look at them," Oscar said. He grabbed Brandon's arm and forced him to stand and look at the car. A passenger in the Toyota leaned out the window and tossed a beer bottle back at the truck. It smashed against the top of the cab and burst. Brandon covered his face but felt the spray of beer and glass hit him. "You think they don't deserve everything we can give them?"

"Fuck you," Ernie called. Then, Oscar started throwing whatever he could find at the car. He started with the beer bottles, then leaned down and grabbed random stuff from the bottom of the truck. Brandon sat on the toolbox again and stared as Oscar tossed a bucket, then a handful of gravel. Brandon's stomach rumbled, sweat broke out on his brow, his fear grew. His dad would owe him more than he ever knew. He kept a death grip on the edges of the toolbox and didn't get up even when Oscar motioned him to move. He motioned again, then when Brandon still didn't move, Oscar pulled him up by the hood of his sweatshirt. "What the fuck's wrong with you, kid?"

Brandon looked down and saw Oscar pulling tools from the box and hurling them at the car. First, a few socket wrenches, then a screwdriver. They were shiny, never used. Brandon's mouth moved, but he couldn't speak. Oscar reached into the toolbox again and came up with a hammer. He shoved it into Brandon's hand. "Here," he said. "Make yourself useful."

The hammer had real weight to it. Brandon stared at it before looking up to see Oscar watching him. He glanced in the back window of the truck and saw Ernie's eyes on him. He had no choice—he had to make nice. Brandon gripped the hammer and turned toward the car. He swung his arm around and shut his eyes as he released it, but that didn't stop the sound of breaking glass from reaching his ears. He opened his eyes and watched in horror as the Toyota swerved across the road and sideswiped a parked car before the driver regained control. Oscar cheered and slapped Brandon on the back.

"Stop throwing the tools, assholes," Ernie yelled out the cab's back window. "Dad'll fucking kill us." Then he looked at Brandon and smiled. "Nice one," he said.

The truck turned off the main road. Oscar knew to brace himself, but Brandon was thrown to the floor. Ernie chased the Toyota up a steep gravel hill. Oscar whooped and hollered in a frenzy of excitement. He was banging on the roof of the truck's cab, yelling, and tossing trash at the car. Brandon stayed on the floor of the truck bed and tried not to roll around.

Ernie tailed the Toyota for a while, but where the gravel ran out and the road turned to mud, he screeched to a halt and jumped out of the truck. "What's going on?" Brandon asked, sitting up and feeling vaguely nauseous in the suddenly still truck. Ernie stuck his arms in the air and whooped in victory. Oscar jumped up and down, danced around the truck, and pumped his fists in the air. "What's happening?" Brandon asked.

"Take a look, buddy boy," Oscar said.

"Where's the car?" Brandon asked.

"Who the fuck cares?" Oscar yelled.

"Chill," Ernie said. "It's right there, dumbass. Stuck in the mud for the rest of time." He waved his arm toward the woods, but Brandon couldn't see anything in the darkness.

Their own truck sat at the very end of the road. Just past the front bumper was a sea of mud. If Ernie hadn't stopped when he did, they'd be stuck, too. Brandon had no clue how they knew.

A new round of beers was passed around, and the guys crowed in delight as they chugged their drinks. Brandon held his beer but barely sipped it. He didn't see any movement in the direction of the car.

"You know what this means, buddy?" Ernie asked and threw his arm around Brandon's shoulders. "This means we win." He tightened his grip around Brandon and rubbed his knuckles across the top of his head. Brandon squirmed out of the hold.

"Win?"

"They're not getting out of there," Ernie said and started laughing. He grabbed another beer and chugged it too.

"You hear that?" Oscar asked and leaned toward Brandon.

"What?"

"Shhh. Listen."

He fell silent, but there was only the noise of crickets chirping and leaves rustling. There was no sound from the car, only empty air all around them. "Guess someone should have warned them it gets muddy up here," Ernie said, and the two of them laughed again. Brandon tried to smile but couldn't.

Oscar and Ernie fell quiet, staring out into nothing as they drank their beers. The night was cool, quiet, the stars bright. There was still no sound from the Toyota, and the darkness hid the passengers, so Brandon didn't know if there'd been any movement. He stared at Oscar and Ernie, outlined by starlight. They looked mean. He didn't think it had anything to do with those boys or with anything they'd done. They were just mean.

Brandon climbed into the back of the truck, glancing over his shoulder to make sure Ernie and Oscar weren't watching, but they were completely oblivious to him. Like they'd forgotten he was there. Like they were bored with him. Like he bored them. He hoped he did.

Brandon made his way to the toolbox and looked inside. There were all sorts of tools he'd never seen before, as well as lengths of rope and a cordless drill. All new. Some still with tags. He dug deeper and found a small flashlight that he shoved in his pocket. He jumped down from the truck.

Ernie turned at the noise and grinned at Brandon. "They're fucked now."

"What do you mean?" Brandon asked.

"Do you know how far from town we are?" Ernie asked. His eyes were glassy with drink.

Brandon nodded, but Ernie kept talking, as though he were the one who'd grown up here. "Ten miles," he said. "Maybe more."

Brandon said nothing. He tried to control his expression. To hide his fear.

"They'll have to walk. And ten miles is a long fucking way in the dark." Ernie laughed. "They'll learn," he said. "They'll learn. You don't fuck with me." He stepped closer to the truck, stuck his middle finger in the air, said, "No one fucks with Brickton boys."

Brandon looked at the finger, then at Ernie's face. It was hard.

Oscar laughed and danced around the truck. He said, "Those mother fuckers'll learn," then yelled toward the car, "Hope you have a nice walk," and, "You're in so much shit," before jumping in the back of the truck. "Brickton boys rule," he screamed into the darkness.

Ernie opened the driver's side door and got inside.

"Get your ass up here," Oscar called to Brandon.

He looked at the faces in the truck, then toward the darkness. He only had a few seconds while Ernie turned the truck around. Brandon switched on the flashlight and pointed it in the direction he'd last seen the Toyota. At first, he only saw an empty car. Then, the boys' heads popped up inside. They were hiding, but they were alive. Brandon breathed a sigh of relief. Then, one boy raised his head enough for

Brandon to see that his face was covered in blood. Already, it was swollen and hard to see what all was broken, but the boy had to be in some serious pain. He waved his arm, as though calling for help. Brandon turned off his flashlight and jumped back in the truck.

"See you later, fuckers," Ernie yelled. Oscar cheered, but it was halfhearted. He was winding down for the night. Oscar sat down in the bed of the truck as they made their way back to town. He jostled Brandon, trying to find a spot out of the wind, but Brandon didn't say anything. He curled up and crossed his arms over his chest, letting the icy air hit his face. It was ten miles to town, a thirty-minute drive on narrow, winding roads. If Brandon called 911 as soon as Ernie dropped him off, an ambulance could be back out here in an hour. A police officer would come to Brandon's house to question him. He wondered if he'd be arrested. The truck's headlights illuminated the road directly in front of them, but the rest of the world was cloaked in darkness. Oscar closed his eyes, even started snoring, but Brandon kept his eyes open. He wondered how long it would take those boys to walk. He stared up at the stars, through a canopy of branches above the road. It was the clearest sky he'd ever seen. He wondered if his dad would approve of how he'd made nice. He blinked once, twice. Tears leaked from the corners of his eyes. It was the wind, he told himself. Nothing more.

A ROOM WITH A DOOR

———

The fence went up in '91 or '92, and the reason we needed it changes depending on who you ask. Some say that before the fence, we would walk into downtown Morgantown, drink at the bars with the undergrads, then crawl back to our units before morning count. But that doesn't make sense. If the fence were here to keep us in, there wouldn't be so many gaps in it. Others claim that after the neighborhood grew up around the prison camp, people started crossing through rather than walking around. Sometimes, when people got drunk late at night, they'd walk through the middle of our compound and pass out. The guards would find them in the morning. We've also heard that before we wore uniforms, the neighborhood women would get in line with us for dinner and eat a free meal on the government's dime.

Whatever the reason, the fence has been up over twenty years now, and we could walk through the gaps anytime we want, but no one does. Or almost no one. The guards say, "Go. See if I care. I won't even chase you." That's right, they won't. Instead, they'll call the federal marshals, who'll pick us up on the side of the road and tack another five years to our sentence.

Mostly, it's better to stay here and make the best of it. Janie Moss got her GED inside. A few other women can cut hair so good they'll have no trouble getting jobs when they're out. Besides, the food's not half bad, and you don't have to worry about paying the rent. If you have a family, it can get pretty rough, and if you're from out of state, it's worse. But it doesn't even look like a prison here, more like a college campus, what with the manicured lawns and greenhouse. Not that we're allowed to walk on the grass—that'll get us a shot, a write-up they look at when deciding whether we qualify for early release. We don't get to eat the food they grow in the greenhouse either, but it's nice to know something thrives here.

Really, though, it's the noise that gets to you. Picture it: six hundred women, half in each unit. That's three hundred women in one giant room with two tiers. No doors on our bunks, no bars either, though sometimes we wish there were. Girls sticking their heads in when you want to be alone, guards poking through your locker whenever they want. Three hundred women, half of them talking at any one time. It's a dull roar, though no one's yelling. Even at night, it doesn't quiet down. Some snore, others cough in their sleep. Guards walk the floor, their shoes clacking against the concrete, whistling to pass the time. Small noises echo off stone walls. You can't even take a piss to get away from it. You think the bathroom will be quiet in the middle of the night, and you walk in to see four legs under a stall door instead of two, both women moaning. It's enough to drive you mad. By the end of our time here, all any of us really wants is peace and quiet. A room with a door and a little silence. Which isn't asking too much.

We all go a little crazy in here, but Sandy Weston's the only one who's ever done anything about it. Really, this is her story, but she's not here to tell it. She's been gone since '98.

Sandy was in for drugs, though you wouldn't know it to look at her. She didn't have the rotten teeth or pock marks of a meth head, and she didn't have track marks either. When she talked about it, all she said was that she fucked up. "I don't know what good it does to keep me in here," she added. "They could have slapped an ankle bracelet on me and left me in Florida." Instead, they'd dragged her to West Virginia with promises of placing her in RDAP, the drug rehab unit, but when she got here, she pissed clean, and they said she didn't have enough proof she was an addict, even with the drug conviction. Then they kept her here, and all her friends in Florida forgot about her, and if she had any family, they never did come see her. So, while the rest of us crowded around for mail call at 6:00, Sandy got one of the good seats in front of the TV and watched the news if they played it or reruns of Jeopardy if the guards blacked the news out that night, which could happen for any number of reasons but usually meant that a former guard was being indicted for sleeping with inmates or bringing in contraband.

Sandy wasn't sad the way some people are when the outside world forgets about them. She said she could even get along inside if she just had a little quiet. "Hell," she said, "I even like West Virginia." She said it wasn't as humid as Florida, and you got a view. "I could live here," she said. "In Morgantown, not prison. I could be happy here, if I could just hear my own thoughts."

The prison is in the middle of a rundown neighborhood on the outskirts of Morgantown, but the town's surrounded by hills covered in trees that turn red and orange and yellow in the fall, blazing for a good month before the leaves die and snow blankets everything you see.

Janie was from the area and said, "I might stay here when I get out. It's a good town." That was just talk. Janie had a fifteen-year sentence, but we didn't remind her that she'd still be here long after most of us were gone. Janie told us she was married, or divorced, or widowed. She either had no kids or five. When she got out, she either had a huge family to return to or no one. Sometimes, if we got bored, we'd ask Janie to tell us about her life, never knowing which story she'd share. Janie liked to embellish the truth. She said Morgantown was home, when she'd grown up fifty miles south. None of her lies hurt anyone, and we figured they were just a way to pass the time. People liked her as long as they took her tales with a grain of salt.

"We could get a house," Sandy said to her. "Roommates."

The two women made plans, decided they'd have a two-bedroom house with a giant porch and turn their entire front yard into a flowerbed that Janie would plant each spring. They settled on marigolds because their oranges and reds blazed like the leaves on the trees in the fall. They were just pipe dreams, but their plans helped to pass the time. Janie wanted a dog, and Sandy said it should be a golden retriever. They decided to name it Rudy and buy it a red collar that would match the color they planned to paint their house.

"It'll happen," Janie said when anyone pointed out that Sandy would be free years before her, long enough to start a life and forget all her prison promises, which never mean much on the outside anyway. "You just watch."

It was a Wednesday morning, and someone had snitched to a guard that there were two cell phones floating around the unit. As soon as count was over, they told us to sit on the floor, backs against the wall. For the next two hours, we watched as they emptied our lockers, checked extra uniforms for hidden pockets, and pulled our four-inch thick mattresses from the metal stands that were bolted to the walls. They snaked toilets and threatened to strip search us. For their trouble, the guards found ten cartons of cigarettes, a bottle of diet pills, hair bleach, and a bottle of nail polish. Even our contraband was boring. The whole time, we cat-called the guards when their backs were turned, whistled under our breath, and mumbled to our neighbors. When the noise level got too high, the guards yelled for us to shut up, and we would quiet down, but the din never ended. It just got muffled for a few minutes before the volume rose again.

One by one, they patted us down before we could leave for lunch, our entire morning wasted. Every time they had to stop to lead a woman off for a strip search, Sandy lost it a little. The room got louder, and people didn't even pretend to be quiet. "You're treating us like prisoners!" someone yelled from the back of the line, which got a burst of laughter. Others called out comments, hoping for another round of giggles, but pretty soon yells overlapped, and sounds bounced around the room, filling every corner and crack. Sandy squatted on the floor, hands over her ears, eyes squeezed shut. Her lips moved silently. No one noticed her for a while, and once we did, no one bothered her. As the line moved forward, we walked around her, careful not to get too close.

People lose it in here sometimes. Not like in the movies where one inmate stabs another with a sharpened toothbrush or attacks a guard. We're not violent. Sometimes there are fights, but that's usually over a woman stealing someone's girlfriend or ratting another person out for contraband. When we can't deal with this place anymore, we do like Sandy: sink down on our heels, rock back and forth, and pretend prison is a bad dream. Or refuse to get out of bed for days until one of our roommates complains to a guard because we're beginning to smell. If we are violent, it's only toward ourselves.

As the last inmate left, Sandy was still huddled on the floor, and she probably got her moment of silence, but the guards wouldn't have let her stay there long. They wanted lunch too.

Later, we heard Sandy was in the SHU, segregated housing. The women who'd been caught with contraband were there too and said they heard crying coming from her cell, but by the time she was back in gen pop the next day, you'd never have guessed she'd been gone. That's the way it is—if you have to lose it, that's fine. Have your meltdown. But don't let it last too long. Instead, you break a little, let the tears come out of the cracks you've formed, and then seal them back up before anyone gets the idea to ship you out. We have it good here, as far as prisons go. If you get shipped, chances are it won't be to a place so good. There, the fence won't have gaps, and the leaves will turn brown and wither, if there are trees at all.

Those of us here long enough to remember Sandy swear she wasn't different the day after her meltdown. Even people who weren't here then claim she ate breakfast and didn't complain when she went to work. All we have are stories, and we share them. Sometimes we borrow a story and make it ours. It's about survival. An inmate who was here then said Sandy swept the floors in cosmetology like it was any other day. Maybe she was quieter than usual, or she could have been more withdrawn, but no one saw reason for alarm. People retreat inside themselves all the time, and it takes more than covering your ears with your hands before anyone worries.

No one saw her at lunch, but Janie Moss swore Sandy returned to the unit in the afternoon. Janie said Sandy took a nap, but none of us really believed that. We all tell tall tales, but you've got to make sure yours ring true, and the idea of Sandy lying down for the afternoon doesn't fit with what happened after. We shrugged Janie's claim off, like we did most of what she said.

It wasn't until 4 p.m. count that anyone noticed something was wrong. First, a guard called Sandy over the intercom, and we knew she'd get a shot if she didn't report. Then, we were all recalled to our units. The guards never had found the rumored cell phones, and we groaned at the thought of another search. They had us line up for an unscheduled count. They were one short.

It's not like in the movies where the siren goes off and guards take off running while we're locked into our cells. In real life, guards searched the compound first. Then, when they didn't find Sandy, they called the marshals, like they said they would. We aren't in here for murder or battery. Those inmates have fences with razor wire and guard towers. We're drug mules and embezzlers. The only thing we could do on the outside is get high or take someone's money. The only thing Sandy's escape would cause is a lot of paperwork.

We whispered for a couple days. After all, Sandy was three years through a five-year sentence. She'd made it over the hump, and when they caught her, she'd pay with another five tacked onto the end. We never considered they wouldn't pick her up. She wouldn't return to our camp—they'd take her somewhere worse, where she couldn't slip out through the gaps in the fence.

Some said she'd gone to the loading docks after lunch and slipped around the back of a delivery truck. Others claimed she'd snuck through a hole in the fence near cosmetology. But Janie Moss said she walked through the front gate, head up, shoulders back, not even pretending to hide. Back then, everyone laughed at Janie, but now, hers is the version we tell new people, especially when they show off, pretend they didn't freeze up and confess every sin they'd ever committed when the marshals ganged up on them in interrogation. We say, "Sandy had more guts than you ever thought of having."

Of course, we assumed she'd been picked up, that she got a day or two on the outside at most. We hoped she'd found someplace quiet to hole up, that she soaked in enough silence to last her the next seven years. And we never would have known any different, as the guards never said another word about her.

But a few weeks after the great escape, once everyone stopped talking about Sandy because there was nothing new to add, Janie said, "I saw Sandy, and you'll never guess where." Nothing better to do, we followed her behind the greenhouse, and she pointed beyond the prison fence to a little house with a porch wider than the building and broken windows covered with garbage bags. "She's in there," Janie said. There was no sign of movement.

"No way," someone said.

"Wait," Janie said. "She'll come out."

We waited. Because what else did we have to do? Prison time is spent watching the calendar, getting through each day the best we can until they tell us we can go home. Staring at a house until someone came out would cross a few more minutes off our sentences.

There were probably ten of us there that day, though to hear the same story a year later, there were fifty, all squatted down behind the greenhouse, a careful fifteen yards from the fence, just beyond the out-of-bounds zone. If anyone in the neighborhood had come outside, they would have wondered what the hell was going on—grown women star-ing at an empty house. But no one else on the street was home, or no one cared. Nice neighborhoods don't sprout up around prisons. Here, rent's low, and the houses are old and falling apart. The families get food stamps and send their kids to school for free lunch.

We sat there for almost an hour, our knees cramping up, ready to laugh at Janie, sure this was another of her lies. Then, the door opened, and a woman stepped out. She had Sandy's brown hair, but it was cut short. Tall and too thin, knees and elbows knobby—just like Sandy. She looked in our direction, but her eyes traveled over and past us.

"Sandy," Janie whispered.

It was. Sandy, wearing shorts and a tank top, sweeping the front porch, then taking a paint scraper to the banister, scraping the old away and making it fresh again.

We didn't move. Didn't breathe. We watched her for an hour until she put the scraper down and walked back inside without even glancing at us.

By lights out, every woman on the compound knew Sandy was living across the street. A few tried to tell the guards, but they waved us away. "You don't need to worry about Sandy," they said. "She's already taken care of." Most women believed them and chalked her sighting up to being another one of Janie's tall tales. The guards must have thought so too, because they never were suspicious of the stories. Instead, they rolled their eyes, Janie's lies legendary.

The next day, a group of us took our knitting behind the green-house, and our needles clicked as we stared at the house. "Why there?" a few of the guards asked, suspicious, and we said it was quieter there than anywhere else on the compound. Aside from the women working in the greenhouse or in the gardens outside, it was mostly silent. After a week or so, the guards stopped asking questions and just did a regular sweep through the area to make sure we weren't sneaking cigarettes or drugs. It was a perfect spot for someone in a car to toss contraband over the fence, but we wouldn't have ruined such a good place. We never were sure if the guards suspected what we were really up to, but we couldn't ask. Instead, we created a knitting club that met every morning behind the greenhouse. We left for meals and again for count, and some of us had to go to work or attend classes, but all day long, a group of us sat there and knitted blankets and scarves to send home or sell to other inmates.

We never reacted when Sandy came out, but we watched her every move. Already, she'd scraped most of the loose paint from the front of the house, and restacked the cinder blocks that made up the stairs. There were even a couple of lawn chairs on the porch, and once each day, Sandy walked out and sat in one. She lit a cigarette and stared at us, but she never waved or smiled. We never called her name or tried to get her attention. We watched. When she ground out her cigarette butt, she stood and went inside.

Sandy's routine never changed, and neither did ours. Prison life is one of waiting. You wait for lunch, for count, for quiet, for freedom. Sandy finished scraping her house and painted it red. She replaced the windows and planted a flowerbed full of marigolds each spring. After a few years, she put a new mailbox up, a miniature of her own house that she must have had specially made. Another few years, and she added black shutters to the house and bird feeders to the trees. She still smoked cigarettes on her porch, and we still watched her. A couple years ago, Sandy stopped dying her hair, and it grew out a pretty shade of silver.

Over the years, who we are has changed. A lot of the women who were here the day she escaped have been released, and a few have died. The space behind the greenhouse is the official spot for the knitting and crochet club, and the grass is worn away from our years of watching. When a new girl comes in and talks about escape, we point to Sandy. "She did it," we say, "and she did it with class." A lot of people here now have never heard of Sandy or her escape. Not everyone makes it into the club.

Recently, a car pulled up in front of Sandy's house just as the sun was setting, while she smoked her cigarette, and we watched as a woman stepped out. There were only three of us still left in prison from the day Sandy escaped. Janie had been released just months earlier, though the rest of the people from that day had been gone for years.

The woman ascended the stairs. She wore red heels the same shade as the house, but a hat hid her face. No one moved, not us or Sandy. The woman sat down in the other chair on the porch, the one that Sandy had put there years before but had always stood empty. She took a cigarette from Sandy's pack and lit it. If they talked, we couldn't hear them, and they didn't look at each other. Instead, they smoked and looked in our direction, though both faces were lost in shadows.

When she finished her cigarette, the woman ground it out and stood. Sandy did too and took a step toward her. They hugged, one of those embraces where you hold onto the other person like you'll drown if it ends. Then, the woman let go. She stepped off the porch. We waited for her to get in the car, but she popped the trunk and pulled out a suitcase. Sandy opened the front door, and light fell on both their faces.

Sandy's lack of surprise at her arrival, the extra chair that looked like it had been waiting for her all these years—it made sense. The new woman was Janie. We watched them both step through the door, and then they were gone.

We turned and walked back to our units, to the world as we knew it, where the guards wouldn't yell when our voices rose, where they wouldn't stop the whispers moving among us. The guards would let us have our stories. They always have. They know we need them.

WINNERS

———

Augie Waller walked toward Ruth with a paper bag from the IGA held high above his head. "I got a bumper crop for you," he said, his voice loud and jubilant.

Ruth grabbed the bag and peered inside—a big pile of squirrel tails. She grinned at him. "These are perfect." She sat at a picnic table on the edge of the play area, her daughter Sophie playing with Gancy, Beth and Augie's youngest, under the slide. The Wallers' boys ran around the play area with another group of kids they'd just met and become immediate friends with, the way some kids do.

The trip to the park was a weekly ritual for Ruth and the Wallers. As soon as the snow melted in the spring and until the first flakes fell in the fall, they met here on Sunday afternoons. Ruth always brought a packet of hotdogs and buns and passed them to Augie, who added them to his family's. Then, Ruth sat with Beth and watched over the kids, breaking up fights when necessary and gossiping about their neighbors. Today, she kept one eye on the paper bag and wondered if she'd have enough tails.

"You got all you need?" Beth asked. She and Augie lived next door to Ruth, and the two of them sometimes sat on their porches and talked once their kids were asleep. Then, when Augie returned from the evening shift at the mines, Ruth sat on her porch alone, smoking cigarette after cigarette until she was exhausted enough to sleep. Sometimes when it was very quiet, she heard Augie and Beth talking or making love through the thin walls of their house. That was when she felt most alone. Not that she wanted Augie. God, no. He was short and portly and balding, his penchant for plaid shirts buttoned tight at his neck a turnoff. What she wanted was their sense of togetherness. The way they belonged to one another. Ruth and Sophie belonged to one another too, but it was different. Augie and Beth and their three kids all relied on one another. They had choices. Ruth and Sophie clung to one another, the only person either one of them had in the world.

"I hope so," Ruth said. Tonight, she'd go through Sophie's toy box to find the squirrel tails Augie had given her last weekend. Then, she could get to work. Spirit week at Brickton Elementary began the next day, and Ruth had promised Sophie something special for Hat Day. Last year, Augie and Beth's daughter, Gancy, had won the competition with a papier-mâché raccoon that sat atop her head. Which wasn't really fair, as it wasn't a hat, more of a sculpture. This year, Ruth was determined Sophie would win with a hat covered in squirrel tails that were arranged to look like raccoon tails to match the school's mascot.

She had the idea two Sundays ago, when Augie had showed up with a grocery bag full of tails that he'd passed out to the kids. They ran around trailing those tails behind them, tickling each other with them, the girls tucking them into their ponytail holders and showing off their extensions. For a whole day after the tails were amputated, they still bent, the vertebrae moving individually. Later, the sinews dried and hardened. Then, Sophie and the others had lost interest, and Ruth had collected them before leaving.

She'd asked Augie for as many tails as he could bring this week but hadn't announced why she needed them, not wanting him to jeopardize

Sophie's chances by his not getting enough of them or his conveniently forgetting. It was stupid, Ruth knew, to compete with Augie and Beth. To compete over something as dumb as whose kid won spirit week. They were her neighbors, had lived next door for years, and they helped her out when she needed it, like when her car wouldn't start or when a foot of snow fell overnight in January. Then, she'd wake to see Augie had dug out her car along with his and Beth's. They were her friends, and Gancy and Sophie were best friends.

Ruth thought about grabbing Sophie and heading home, but the chill air reminded her that these Sundays at the park wouldn't last much longer. Once the first snowflakes started to fall, these days with her neighbors and her evenings with Beth would come to an end, and the long winter would be ahead of her. That was always a hard time of year, watching Augie and Beth and their three kids do family things, while she tried to be enough family for Sophie on her own.

Beth didn't work and drove her kids to and from sports and clubs and lessons, while Ruth worked full-time and had Sophie ride the bus from school to the dentist's office where she was a hygienist. There, her daughter looked at the same *Highlights* magazines day after day, finding the same animals hidden in some artist's rendering for the tenth time. Sometimes, when Beth had a fun event planned for Gancy, like a day at the splash pad, she invited Sophie to join them, but Ruth only agreed to let her go occasionally. When Sophie returned home from an exciting outing that Gancy took for granted, Ruth could see the naked envy in her daughter's eyes. Only six, and already she was learning how unfair life was, and that broke Ruth's heart. So, most of the time she kept Sophie with her, sheltering her from all the things she was missing, trying to make their life enough.

Now, Augie was at the grill, coaxing the coals to life, and Beth pulled paper plates from a battered grocery bag. Ruth sat back and watched the boys stand to the side and whisper in one another's ears, staring at Sophie and Gancy in a way that let Ruth know they'd soon upset the girls' game. Sophie reached up, scratched her head. Then, again.

"Sophie," Ruth called, and her daughter turned to her. "Stop scratching."

She nodded, turned back to Gancy, and scratched again. The boys were still whispering.

"Sophie," Ruth yelled, louder this time. "Stop that."

Sophie stood, looking at her mother, one hand absentmindedly scratching at her scalp. "There's something in my hair," she said. She walked toward Ruth, still scratching. "It itches."

"It's sand," Ruth said. When they'd arrived at the playground, Sophie had immediately headed for the sandbox, letting Gancy bury her. Since then, she'd been scratching.

"Sand doesn't hurt," Sophie said.

Ruth bent her ear forward and saw black spots. Almost like pepper flakes, but they were eggs. Which would hatch into lice. Some already crawled through Sophie's hair and across her scalp.

"I don't see anything," Ruth said. Her voice was high, breathless.

"But it itches," Sophie said. She used both hands now, scratching furiously.

"Stop it," Ruth said. She grabbed her daughter's hands, pinned them to her sides.

"Let go, Mom." Sophie tried to wriggle out of Ruth's grasp.

"We're leaving," Ruth whispered. "You can scratch all you want in the car."

"I don't wanna go," Sophie said, her lower lip poking out. "We were playing a game."

Ruth looked at Beth and Augie, busy preparing lunch. The last thing Ruth needed was their blaming her for a lice outbreak in the neighborhood. Saying she was too busy to keep her daughter clean. Saying she needed to spend more time at home. Not that they'd say it. But they'd think it.

"We're leaving," she repeated quietly. Sophie started crying, big blubbery sobs, and Beth was looking at her now. "We have to go," Ruth said.

"Is everything okay?" Beth called.

"What about your lunch?" Augie asked. He held up her package of hotdogs.

"We're okay," Ruth said. "I forgot something. We're supposed to be somewhere. You can eat our dogs."

She grabbed Sophie's hand, but the girl sank to the ground, tears spilling down her cheeks, sobs wracking her entire body. Beth and Augie were staring now. Ruth bent down, picked up her daughter, and started for the car, Sophie screaming, "I don't wanna. I don't wanna." Halfway there, Ruth remembered the squirrel tails, almost decided to leave them, then thought better of it. She ran back, her arms still wrapped around Sophie's writhing body, grabbed the bag, and walked back to her car, her eyes locked on where she needed to be, not on her neighbors' gaze.

She heard Beth call, "You sure everything's okay?" but didn't answer. Sweat ran between Ruth's breasts and down her back. Her face was red. They'd talk about her after she left, but that was the least of her worries. She hated lice, the pain that went along with getting rid of the nits. Tears filled her eyes, but she blinked them away. She could get through this. They were just bugs.

She buckled Sophie into her booster seat and waved at the Wallers, who were watching her, Augie still holding the hotdogs, before she jumped into the driver's seat. She backed out and sped away from the parking lot, driving two blocks before pulling onto a side road and stopping the car. Sophie wailed in the back seat, gasping sobs that shook her whole body. Ruth took an antiseptic wipe from her purse and ran it over her hands, in between her fingers, and up her forearms. She tried not to think about the shampoo and fine-toothed comb and medicinal smell still awaiting her.

When she was ten, Ruth had gone to her own mother complaining of an itchy head. Her mom had found a mass of lice in Ruth's hair, her scalp red and raw from bites and scratching, lice eggs covering the folds of her ears. "Only dirty girls get lice," her mother had said. "No daughter of mine is going to be a dirty girl." After a trip to the drugstore, Ruth had sat in the tub and cried while her mother scrubbed her head with foul-smelling shampoo and then forced a metal comb with sharp teeth through her hair. By Ruth's bedtime her mother had run out of patience. She pulled a pair of scissors from her sewing box and cut chunks out of her hair until it was all gone and her scalp showed through in places.

In the morning, Ruth woke to find clumps of hair still on the bathroom floor. When she looked in the mirror, she cried. Her mom blamed Ruth for the haircut, said if she weren't so dirty, she wouldn't have been forced to do it. Then, she cried too and took Ruth to a salon in the mall for a woman to fix it, but there wasn't a lot the hairdresser could do. "Come back when it grows out a bit," she'd said.

Ruth wouldn't leave Sophie with those same mental scars. She would shampoo her daughter's hair and comb it again and again, as many times as she had to. And she wouldn't dig the teeth of the comb into her daughter's scalp. She'd be gentle. Her own daughter wouldn't be traumatized.

Now, along with her wailing, Sophie had begun to kick Ruth's seat. "Stop it," Ruth screamed, and for a moment Sophie was silent. But her tantrum wasn't over, only on pause. The little girl took a gulp of air before continuing her assault on Ruth's eardrums and kidneys.

"We can't go to the park," Ruth said quickly. "But I'll get you a treat if you'll just shut up." The last words came out higher pitched than she'd intended, but they seemed to have gotten through.

Sophie sniffled, gulped, said quietly, "What kind of treat?"

"What kind do you want?" Ruth asked.

"An Icee," Sophie said. "From the Pantry Store."

Ruth never let her have Icees, said they were pure sugar and had no nutritional value. Instead, she made smoothies that Sophie always bemoaned as not tasting as good as she thought an Icee would.

"Deal," Ruth said, and quick as that, her daughter's feet stopped drumming against the back of her seat. Ruth took a deep breath, felt the crazy need to run from her daughter disappear. She pulled back onto the road.

When she stopped in front of the store, Sophie started to unbuckle her seat belt, but Ruth held up her hand. "You stay here."

"Why?"

"You have lice," Ruth said. "I don't want you to give it to everyone."

"What's lice?"

"Bugs," Ruth said. "You have bugs in your hair."

Sophie began to sniffle again. "Bugs?" she asked, her voice watery with tears.

"It's okay, though," Ruth said quickly. "We'll fix them when we get home. But first, you're going to get an Icee."

* * *

Ruth sat beside the bathtub, dishwashing gloves on her hands, as she worked the shampoo into Sophie's hair. After stopping at the Pantry Store, they'd gone to the drugstore, where Ruth had bought a gallon of bleach and all five bottles of lice shampoo, unsure that one would be enough. Sophie's hair covered in suds was step one of her plan, which involved washing Sophie's sheets and pillowcases, boiling her hairbrush and throwing away her ponytail holders. After that, she'd wash all of Sophie's clothes. And for good measure, all the towels and her own bedding and all of her clothes. Everything, really. Then, she'd wipe down the whole house with bleach. Once everything was disinfected, Ruth planned to wash her own hair in the special shampoo.

"It stinks," Sophie said.

"It used to burn too," Ruth said. The memory of the heat on her scalp made her cringe. "Consider yourself lucky."

She shook a sweaty lock of hair out of her eyes. This was the fourth time she'd applied the shampoo. The bottle said not to do it more than once in a day, but Sophie had so much hair Ruth didn't know what else to do.

"Tilt your head back," she said and turned on the spigot. She held Sophie's head under the water, careful to keep the suds out of her eyes. Her phone rang again, the fourth time since they'd arrived home. Ruth glanced at the screen, where it sat on the lid of the toilet. Beth. Again. She'd have to answer it soon, or else she'd start knocking on the front door.

"Can I get it?" Sophie asked and started to reach for it, but Ruth slapped her hand away.

"One more time with the comb," she said.

"Do we have to?" Sophie asked. She'd been in the tub for two hours. Her fingers and toes were shriveled like raisins.

"Unless you want me to cut all your hair off."

Sophie turned her back to Ruth and let her coax the comb through her wet hair. She screeched when it hurt too badly and sobbed a few times, but Ruth thought she did a good job. Still, her daughter had too much hair—there was no way she could get all the nits out. At least not today. Already, there were red splotches on Sophie's scalp, where the comb had bitten into her skin. Ruth had sworn she'd be careful, but it wasn't easy. She could see the little black dots on her daughter's head, and she had to scrape them with the comb to dislodge the eggs.

Sophie began to cry again, and Ruth sighed. They were both tired. She'd already done three loads of laundry, and she hadn't gotten to her own bedding yet. Never mind wiping the entire house down with bleach. "That's enough for now," she said. "We'll try again tomorrow."

Sophie jumped up, and Ruth wrapped her in a towel that hung almost to the floor. "You did good," she said and watched her daughter run down the hallway, her lice infested hair trailing to her waist. Ruth was beginning to understand why her mom had cut off her own hair. It took everything in her not to take a pair of scissors to Sophie's head and make this whole thing a little easier.

* * *

After she loaded all the towels into the washing machine and wiped the entire bathroom down with bleach and took all the clothes out of her own dresser and closet and stripped her bed and decided that she'd have to take her comforter to the laundromat in the morning, Ruth approached Sophie's bedroom door with a garbage bag and a rag in a bucket of bleach water. It was ten o'clock, and her eyes burned from the chemicals in the air. She hadn't made dinner, but when Sophie complained about hunger, she'd handed her a box of cookies. Now, Sophie sat on her mattress clad only in underwear and cookie crumbs. She held two Barbies. They were fighting each other, and two more lay on the floor, their heads gone.

Ruth knew she should say something, but instead she grabbed the two from the floor and wiped their naked bodies down with bleach before putting them back on her daughter's bed. "They had lice," Sophie said. "I fixed it." She pointed to the toy box, where their heads lay atop a heaping pile of toys. Sighing, Ruth knelt in front of the box. If she could finish Sophie's room tonight, she could spend all day tomorrow cleaning the rest of the house. She'd already called into work.

She grabbed the Barbie heads, saw that they didn't really have lice, and wiped them down before tossing them onto the bed where Sophie now played with their headless bodies. "They're all better now," Ruth said. She turned back to the box and pulled the toys out one by one.

Anything made of plastic got wiped down and put in a pile on the floor. All the stuffed animals went into a separate pile that would go into the washing machine. Ruth had no clue if they would survive the washing, and she didn't really care. Her head thumped and her whole body ached. She wanted to take a shower and crawl into bed, but all she could think of was the lice waiting for her there. She was probably covered in bugs already.

Any toys Sophie hadn't played with in recent memory went into the garbage bag. Ruth came to a squirrel tail, then another. She remembered the hat and swore under her breath. The other tails were still in the trunk of her car. Slowly, she stood, her knees creaking.

Outside, Beth sat on Ruth's front steps, wrapped in one of Augie's plaid shirts, cradling a cup of coffee between her palms. "I knocked," she said.

"I didn't hear you." Which was the truth, though Ruth didn't say that she probably wouldn't have answered even if she'd heard.

"Are you okay?" Beth asked. "We were worried sick when you took off so fast."

"We're fine," Ruth said. Beth looked expectant, as though waiting for more of a response. Ruth didn't have the energy to make something up, so she said nothing.

"You look like hell," Beth said.

Ruth looked down at the stained sweatpants that hugged her hips too tightly, the paint splattered t-shirt with sweat rings under her arms. She imagined her face and hair looked just as ravaged. "I feel like hell," she said and walked down the front steps, to her car parked on the street, and pulled out the bag of squirrel tails.

"What did you need those for?" Beth asked, nodding at the bag.

"A hat," Ruth said. "For Sophie. It's spirit week at school."

Beth smiled. "Gancy loved her hat last year."

"She won."

"What?" Beth was standing now, ready to leave Ruth's porch, but she paused.

Ruth held the paper bag against her chest and looked up at her friend. "She won the contest."

"She didn't win," Beth said and walked down the steps. She leaned against the retaining wall, arms crossed over her chest. "There aren't any winners for spirit week."

"What do you mean?"

"It's not a competition," Beth said. A smash and screech sounded from the other side of her closed front door. She moved toward her house, saying over her shoulder, "I should go before they kill each other." She stopped before walking inside, said, "If you want to talk," and Ruth nodded.

Once the door closed, Ruth said, "Yes, it is," but of course Beth didn't hear.

Ruth hugged the paper bag more tightly, suddenly angry. She took a deep breath, then another, felt the anger grow. It *was* a competition. And the only reason Beth didn't know that was because she was winning. When you win without trying, you don't have to compete. Everyone else does. People like Ruth do.

* * *

In the weak morning light, with barely three hours of sleep, her fingers and thoughts both shaky from too much coffee, Ruth sat at the kitchen table facing a ball cap with the Pantry Store logo on the foam front, the Brickton Bandits logo cut from an old t-shirt, a bottle of fabric glue, a pile of stiffened squirrel tails from Sophie's toy box, the bag of fresh ones from Augie, and a staple gun. She got to work covering the original logo with the new one, smoothing the edges so you could barely tell she was repurposing the hat. That done, she turned to the squirrel tails, stapling them to the sides of the bill and all the way around the mesh cap. When she ran out of tails, she opened the paper sack and saw that Augie had outdone himself—there were piles of tails, enough to overlap them so you wouldn't be able to tell one from the next, so they'd cover Sophie's hair completely.

She reached in and grabbed a handful. When she laid them on the table, Ruth spotted something odd and leaned forward, her nose almost touching the tails. Then, she reared back so quickly she almost fell over, the chair skittering out behind her and clattering to the floor. Hand to her chest, breathing too fast, Ruth was suddenly standing on the other side of the room, her back against the formica countertop. Slowly, she crept forward, trying to see without getting too close. Then, she spotted it. Bugs. Nits. All over the squirrel tails.

She slapped the table with the palm of her hand. "Dammit, Augie," she said. "I knew my baby wasn't dirty." She grabbed a garbage bag from under the sink, ready to dump the whole thing in unceremoniously. Screw the hat. Screw spirit week.

Then, she stopped.

Sophie already had lice. No matter how much Ruth had washed and bleached last night, Sophie's hair was too long and too thick. It didn't much matter whether she wore the hat to school or not. So, Ruth pulled her own hair back more securely, grabbed her dishwashing gloves again, and got to work.

HOUSE OF TIRES

———

It was four in the morning when the Subaru jumped the curb and crashed through the plate glass window, overturning piles of tires that were balanced for visual effect. Ned was in the garage. By the time the car stopped, it was inside the showroom. A woman stumbled out, a knot already rising on her forehead where her head had hit the windshield, a red mark from the steering wheel across her neck.

"Oh, shit," she said. "I can't get a DUI."

Ned looked at the car in the middle of his showroom and the skid marks across the floor. He calculated the cost of the repair, imagined a parade of people stopping by to see the car. "You could go," he said.

"What?"

"Go. Sober up. I won't call the cops, and you'll pay for the window and sign the car over to me."

The car was a bucket of bolts, held together with duct tape and dumb luck. It was twenty years old if it was a day, and if the floorboards weren't already rusted through, they would be soon. But Ned didn't plan to drive it. House of Tires was new, and he needed the publicity. Otherwise, he'd spend the rest of his life coming to work at three in the morning and falling into bed at midnight, never making a cent off the place.

The garage had only been open a couple of years, Ned's present to himself for his fortieth birthday. Since he was fifteen, he'd worked in other people's garages and dreamed of being the boss. Until he was, and so far it wasn't what he'd expected. Business wasn't booming, and according to his books, he was six months away from going belly up.

"Deal," the woman said, and they shook hands. Before she left, Ned took her license as guarantee that she'd return with the title later in the day. Or he'd call the cops. Either would work.

And she did return, though he didn't recognize her at first. In the morning, her face had been smeared with makeup, eyes watery and red-rimmed, her hair a mess of tangles. The woman who arrived a few hours later was perfectly groomed, tight jeans, a tucked-in Harley Davidson t-shirt hugging her breasts, eyes bright, a small smile on her lips. "Hey there," she said, and he did a double-take. She laughed. "I know."

She brought someone with her, a man Ned found himself disliking until he started measuring the window frame, leafing through the pages of a binder. "Glass or plexiglass?" he asked Ned.

"Glass," he said. The guy nodded and began adding up figures. Not a husband, then. Or a boyfriend. Not that Ned was interested. He didn't have time for distractions—he had a business to build. Besides, she was a drunk, had driven a car through his garage and then was brazen enough not even to be ashamed when she returned. But he had to admit there was an edge to her.

She stood in front of him, hand on a hip she cocked to the side, while the man did his calculations. Finished, he glanced up from a sheet of paper, stated a number that seemed way too high, but the woman opened her purse and pulled out a wad of money. She licked her thumb and pulled some bills off, passing them to the man. She turned to Ned. "My license?"

He glanced at it as he pulled it from the register, wishing he'd paid more attention earlier. Now, all he saw was the state: Pennsylvania. He wondered how often she made it down to Brickton. He wondered if she'd be back. "See you around," she said as she walked out, hips swinging the whole way. He watched her cross the street, pass the post office, then turn the corner by the Pantry Store, where she disappeared. Ned sighed, shook himself. The woman was already an apparition. Someone he'd have grown up with if she were from Brickton, whose childhood home would be as familiar as his own, who he'd have dated in high school, possibly slept with, and have long since written off as too wild.

He returned to his work, sweeping up the shards of glass, restacking the tires, and putting a sign on the car that said, "Need brakes? Ned's House of Tires has you covered!" Then he had the window replaced, the Subaru still inside his shop. People stopped by for the next week to see the car that had plowed through the front of the store. While they were there, they went ahead and had their brakes checked and their tires rotated. Even the police stopped by, but they weren't going to write up a complaint. Besides, they said, he could have driven the car in himself and pretended someone else had. There was no proof a crime had been committed. Ned began to wish there were, that he'd refused to return her license, that he'd demanded dinner with her in exchange for not calling the cops, that he'd just plain asked her out. No matter how often he told himself he didn't need that kind of drama in his life, he couldn't get the sway of her hips out of his mind.

From that day on, the House of Tires was the place to go for your vehicle's needs in Brickton. People stopped by to see the smashed up car but realized that Ned's work was good and fairly priced. That one accident had allowed him to stop pulling such long hours, to hire another mechanic and someone to help run the business end of the store, a young kid named Charlie Folger who worked hard and didn't talk much. Over the next few months, he built up the business and kept an eye out for the Pennsylvania lady, who he was sure had told him she'd see him around, though he didn't see her anywhere. A few times, he thought he glimpsed her across parking lots or through the shelves of the Dollar General but it was always someone else, so he came to believe he'd never see her again.

And then, like magic, six months after she crashed into his garage, in the wee hours of the morning when Ned stopped by the Pantry Store for a package of those little powdered doughnuts, he recognized the curve of the hips, the snug jeans of the woman in front of him. "Subaru lady," he said without thinking, and she actually turned around.

She looked at him blankly. Then, that smile bloomed on her lips, and she said, "My friends call me Lois."

"Lois," he said, enjoying the taste of the syllables. "Ned. Would you like to see that bucket of bolts you left in my garage?"

They walked there slowly, leaving both their cars in the Pantry Store parking lot, asking the expected questions about spouses and kids and jobs, and once they'd admired his display with the Subaru and all it had done for his shop—"I guess now when I tell people, I'll have an end to the story," she said—they sat on the chairs in the waiting area and talked for two hours, until the guys on the morning shift arrived, and he introduced Lois to them as the Subaru lady. "She's the one who made all this possible," he said, waving his arm at the garage.

"I didn't do a thing," she said. "Ned here knew how to turn my stupidity into a gold mine." Then, they made plans for dinner that evening, and it was like everything clicked into place.

The next month went by in a blur—Charlie handled the front of the shop, the guys in the garage worked from sun up to sun down, and Ned barely saw the place, spending all his free time with Lois. She had him taking road trips to the southern part of the state, hiking trails he'd never heard of, eating cotton candy at small town fairs, chasing tequila with PBR at roadside bars. One night, while they were sitting on a swing set in a park Lois had spied from the road, she looked at him, cocked her head in a way that drove him nuts, and said, "Marry me."

"Okay," he said, and even though he knew the whole affair was crazy and it was even crazier to rush into marriage, Ned bought two tickets to Vegas the next day, and they had a drive-thru ceremony with an Elvis dressed in a white sequined jumpsuit. Back in Brickton, Ned put all of Lois's belongings in the back of his truck and moved her into his house, where they fell into a routine of sorts. On Mondays, Ned would go to work, doing a few oil changes or helping with an engine rebuild. Then, at some point that day or the next, Lois would arrive with a map or a brochure for some event. "What's the plan?" he'd say.

"You work too hard," she'd reply, though he never really did. "Let's have an adventure."

And they would, hopping in the truck and driving wherever Lois claimed to have found the next bit of excitement. Business was good enough that Ned could disappear for days and leave the details to Charlie. A full tank of gas and a destination were all he and Lois needed.

They could have survived like that too, just the two of them balancing their lives between a successful garage and adventures in every small town in the tri-state area, enjoying the fruits of his labors. Except someone from outside of Brickton bought a scrap of land across from House of Tires and erected a brick building. "What do you think?" Ned asked Lois when they broke ground.

"Whatever it is," she replied, "will just bring more people to House of Tires." Then they'd left for a weekend trip and hadn't thought of it again. Until they returned to see a giant sign that read "Future Home of Car Crews," a national auto repair chain.

* * *

When Car Crews opened, they hung yellow and red banners out front, announcing one month of five-dollar oil changes. In that month, over half of Ned's customers jumped ship. "Everyone will crawl back when they jack those oil changes up to thirty bucks," Ned said. "They'll have their tails between their legs."

But at the end of the month, Car Crews raised their oil changes to twenty bucks and added on a free tire rotation every other change. Ned couldn't compete, and House of Tires lost a little more business, but he kept the doors open, with a few adjustments. He bought the cheap coffee now and dumped it into an old Maxwell House can. He did more of the work himself, spending longer hours at the shop, telling Lois to make her trips alone. His most loyal customers, those who'd been coming to him from the very beginning, stayed at House of Tires, but most people had jumped ship to save a few pennies.

"It's not fair," he told Lois. "We're home-grown. A chain doesn't care about this town."

They stood inside the showroom. It was late at night. Earlier that evening, Charlie had told them what they already knew: they were losing money faster than they were making it. Some of the mechanics' hours had to be cut. Ned had already laid off two of them, young guys who'd be able to get jobs easily. He worried about the older men. They depended on House of Tires as much as he did.

"We could leave," Lois said.

"What?"

"Take what we have in the store and go." Her eyes shone, and for a moment, Ned saw the drunk woman who'd driven her car through his window.

"No," he said. He moved away from her, laid both his palms on the front counter.

She grabbed his shoulders and leaned into his back. "We could go on the road, have adventures every day. We could get enough for this place so we wouldn't have to work for a couple years if we're careful."

"I made this place," he said. "It's my dream."

"We can make new dreams," she said, and in that moment, he hated Lois just a little bit.

"I can fix this," he said.

"It's just a garage," she said.

Ned turned to face her, put his hands on her shoulders, and slowly pushed her away from him. "Never say that to me again."

The next day, he took out an ad in the paper, complete with coupons. The discounts cut their profit to almost nothing, but Ned figured if they could just get their customers back, they'd find a way to make up the difference. Maybe they could drive the other place out of business, then raise their prices again. School kids held fundraisers in the lot, washing cars to fund their teams. Ned hired the local country station to broadcast live while he announced offers. He hosted a cookout with hamburgers and soda. He manned the grill, while Lois took off on some solo adventure. When she returned that night, her eyes were glassy, and when he asked how much she'd had to drink, she didn't answer.

None of his ideas worked. Car Crews took more of his business every day, and Lois returned later each night.

"We need to go bigger," Ned told her. "We need a gimmick, something to get people from outside of Brickton to come here."

"You need to close the doors and stop while you're ahead."

Ned called the Gazette about a feature, a special interest piece on the old Subaru. He also called a local TV station about filming a commercial but didn't tell Lois. When she saw the full-page ad in the paper, she'd turned to him and said, "I'm not going down with you on this." Which worried Ned. They wouldn't make money if they didn't spend any, but it was hard to tell her that when she already had one foot out the door.

At night, in bed, he and Lois whispered furiously, though they didn't need to whisper, alone in the house. Still, it was like if they spoke too loud, they'd frighten their marriage away.

"This isn't what I signed up for," she said.

"What did you expect?"

"Fun," she said. "The garage is your dream, not mine. It could burn in a fire, and I'd roast marshmallows over the flames. We used to have fun. Now, you pretty much live at House of Tires."

He did. It was like those first months after he'd opened the garage, when business barely trickled in, and Ned did his books over and over, figuring ways to stretch every penny as far as possible. He barely slept, barely ate, spent every waking hour at the garage and ignored the rest of his life. Then, there wasn't much of a life to ignore—the guys at the Elks, buck season. Now, though, he was ignoring Lois, and he'd been hoping she wouldn't bring it up. He wasn't even sure she'd noticed—her adventures took her away more and more, and she came home later and later, often half drunk. "Dammit, Lois," he said. "I'm doing my best."

"Well, your best isn't good enough."

Ned lay on his back, looking up at the ceiling. Lois's breathing was loud and fast in his ear. He could feel her staring at him through the darkness. He closed his eyes, stayed as still as possible, gripped the sheet, pretended to sleep. Eventually, she leaned back, her weight settling onto her side of the mattress. Then, her breathing slowed. Still, he waited until she snored lightly before rising from the bed, going into the kitchen, where he'd look over the books one more time, see what corners he could cut, where he could shave a penny. When all this was over, she'd understand. She'd see that he could give her the life she wanted. He just needed more time.

* * *

When all the coupons and sales and picnics and freebies failed and all the money was long since gone, Ned froze. He couldn't see a way forward, and he couldn't admit that this was the end of House of Tires. So, he did nothing. He showed up to work every morning, him and Charlie who kept coming even though Ned hadn't paid him in weeks. He worked on the one or two cars that might show up, guys who knew him from the Elks stopping by to have their oil changed too often, imagining leaks where there were none, or creating problems for him to fix. And Ned didn't say a thing. He kept his head down, working whatever jobs people threw his way, opening earlier and closing later in hopes that someone would arrive.

At night, Lois placed bills beside his dinner plate but never said a word about them. They were all past due. Some were from collection agencies. She sat across from him, her face drawn. If she was there at all. Some nights, she came home long after he was asleep. He'd find her on the couch in the morning, hung over and silent, never offering an excuse for her absence. And he didn't ask. Didn't want to know, truth be told.

After a week of this, she dropped her fork on her plate. It clanged loudly in the silent kitchen, and Ned looked up, meeting her eyes for the first time in who knows how long. "I think I'm done," she said.

"Done?" He put his fork down.

"I can't do this," she said.

"This?" he asked.

"You're gonna make me say it," she said.

His heart beat faster. "Don't."

"Don't what?"

"Don't go." It hurt his heart to say it like that.

She was already shaking her head.

"I have one more idea," he said. "If it doesn't work, we'll go. We'll get in the truck and go."

"I don't believe you," she said.

"Let me tell you," he said and tried to pull something together in his mind, but she held up her hand.

"I don't want to know." She looked tired, beaten.

"But—" he said.

She stood, her chair scraping against the floor. She held her thumb and index finger an inch apart and leaned toward him. "I'm this far from being done," she said. "This far."

"Thank you," he said, nodding. Trying not to jump out of his chair and hug her. "You won't be sorry."

* * *

The Car Crews sign glowed above the parking lot full of cars. Across the street, House of Tires was dark—there were no cars in the lot, none in the garage. In fact, no one had dropped a vehicle off in two days. Before that, there was a rash of flat tires amongst the guys at the Elks: gashes in the sidewall, nails in the tread, leaking valves, but nothing since then. Even his friends had run out of make believe issues.

It was five in the morning, overcast but cold out. Cars passed by the lot occasionally, but their headlights warned him of their arrival long before they could see him. Ned squatted on the edge of the Car Crews lot, and when the coast was clear he made his way to a sedan. It was old, unlocked, and best of all, someone had hidden a key inside the gas cap door. He slid behind the steering wheel, hoped for a second that the car wouldn't start, but the engine turned over without hesitation. He almost turned it off again, but Lois hadn't come home last night. She hadn't come home the night before either. He didn't have a choice.

He put the car into drive and made his way toward the edge of the parking lot. He looked both ways, but the road was empty, so he turned on the headlights. The car was aimed at House of Tires, and as far as he could tell, right at Lois's Subaru in the showroom. He stepped on the gas. The car gained speed as he exited the lot and crossed the road. It bumped over the curb to the lot without a hitch, his headlights reflecting in the glass of the showroom. Just feet from the window, the reflection was replaced by a view of the whole room—the counter, the stacks of tires, the Subaru, and walking through the middle of it all, Lois.

Ned slammed on the brakes, but it was too late—the car was already breaking through the glass. Lois jumped back. He turned the steering wheel, but he still smashed into the Subaru, sending the pile of tires flying. The Subaru jolted back and slammed into Lois. She fell and disappeared from his view. There was a thump as the car ran over something.

Before he came to a complete stop, Ned had unbuckled his seatbelt and jumped from the car. "Lois," he cried, peering under the front tires, but she lay a few feet away from the front bumper. He thanked his lucky stars she wasn't under the car, until he saw her knee bent in the wrong direction, her arm bent where there was no joint.

He ran to her, crouched over her, touched her cheek, but she jerked back from him. "Don't touch me," she said.

"It's me, Lois," Ned said. "You're safe."

He tried to touch her again, but she scooted back on her good arm, crying out. She was confused. He turned away, saw the car in the middle of the shop, shoved against the old Subaru.

Outside, people were yelling. In the distance, sirens. "I have to go," he said.

"I'm leaving," she said, soft now. She lay back against the tile, her eyes closed.

"You're hurt," he said. "Bad. You can't go anywhere. They'll find you." He squeezed her hand.

"I came to tell you," she said.

"You're talking crazy," he said. "Don't worry. We'll be okay." She didn't respond. The voices were closer now. He stood and ran.

At the doorway to the garage, he turned back, saw the two cars butted up against one another, could already picture the display he'd create, the sea of people stopping by to see the freak occurrence. He and Lois would pose for pictures before taking off on another adventure.

He ducked under one of the bay doors and crossed the lot with his head bowed. It was early still, barely light out, but Brickton was coming to life. People nearby had heard the burst of glass, the crunch of metal on metal, and were peering out windows, jogging toward the garage.

Her car sat on the edge of the lot. He slid behind the wheel, and for once, he loved that she always left the key in the ignition. He glanced in the rearview mirror and saw Lois's belongings piled on the backseat. His heart dropped to his stomach, but he told himself that she'd stay now. She had to.

He drove out of Brickton on side roads, only a few other cars out. He took deep breaths, felt his heartbeat slow. He practiced looking surprised, his eyes wide, his mouth open. He glanced in the mirror, gauged his expression, closed his mouth some, let his lips part just a tiny bit. Better. Ten mile out of town, when his expression was believable, he turned onto Route 250, where he'd be seen heading toward town. No way he was in Brickton during the accident. No way he'd been anywhere near the garage. Halfway back, it occurred to him that Lois might tell, but he shoved that thought away. She was his wife. She wouldn't. She couldn't. He repeated this to himself the rest of the drive. He didn't look in the backseat.

As he neared the garage, he saw yellow tape blocking House of Tires and Car Crews. Police cars and fire crews blocked the road. Ned slowed, then stopped. He switched off the ignition, opened the door, planted his feet on solid earth, ready to react.

* * *

When Ned woke, she was staring at him. "Lois," he breathed and leaned forward. It was his third night in the hospital, and he still wore the clothes he'd had on when he drove into the garage. The police had been in and out, but Lois had remained asleep. The doctors said it was normal, that her head had bounced off the tile floor from the force of the impact, that she would wake up soon. He hadn't left in all that time, was beginning to smell a bit, but he didn't care. He listened as the doctors said soon over and over, but yesterday he'd stopped believing them and told himself that he'd killed his wife. Now though, early in the morning on the third day, her eyes were open, and she stared at him without speaking. "Lois," he said again, louder this time, and leaned forward.

She flinched as he touched her good arm but didn't pull away. Not that she could—she had a cast from her ankle to ass on her left leg, her right arm in another cast, and her whole body was covered in bruises. "I was afraid you'd never wake up."

Still, she said nothing, blinked at him a few times and watched him as though she didn't know who he was.

His eyes filled with tears. Everything would be okay now. He leaned forward, grasped her hand. She didn't pull away, but she didn't respond. "You're okay," he said. Now, the tears spilled over. "It worked," he said. "They're coming back. They've been calling ever since the accident."

"Accident?" she asked.

He ignored that, said, "Charlie can't keep up with the calls. We have appointments lined up for the next two weeks. As soon as you're better, we can go on another adventure. A long adventure." He put his forehead against hers, breathed in the scent of her.

She turned away, toward the window. Outside, the world was gray, overcast.

Ned grabbed her chin, turned her face toward him. "We did it," he said, his triumph turning to frenzy as he searched her face for some reaction. "We did it," he said again, and shook her head slightly. She grimaced, groaned, but he didn't let go. He kept hold of her chin, made her look into his eyes.

Eventually, quietly, sadly, Lois said, "You did it."

FAT BOTTOMED GIRLS

———

Someone plays Queen's "Fat Bottomed Girls" on the jukebox, and the diner's kitchen door swings open to reveal a three-hundred-pound woman wearing pasties, a G-string, and knee-high boots. "Surprise!" she says to Ramsey, who sits on a stool decorated with balloons. Her hair is teased into poufs of blonde, and it looks like she's put her makeup on with a spatula, eyelashes like spiders, eyeliner that ends at her temples, her mouth a smear of red lipstick. Karen, the day manager, grabs Ramsey by the shoulder and says, "Something to remind you of what's waiting at home."

Size-wise, the stripper is similar to Anne Marie but that's as far as the likeness goes, and he's damn sick of Karen comparing every fat woman she sees with his fiancé. He wouldn't even be here if Anne Marie hadn't said, "She really wants to give you a big send-off. The least you can do is show up." Ramsey hadn't had the heart to tell her that the last thing Karen wanted was to wish them well.

So, now he's here, watching everyone laugh as the stripper shoves one man's face after another into her cleavage. Ramsey would rather be at home with Anne Marie, playing poker for nickels or watching a movie, his head cradled in her breasts while she massages his scalp. Instead, he's half drunk on rum and coke in the diner where he spends most of his days. His employees shrink in their seats when the stripper comes near them, willing to pretend but hoping they don't have to. Karen stands behind the ring of chairs, out of reach.

She is tall and bony, with a frown on her face more often than not. It's her fault Ramsey sits here, waiting for the night to be over. When he told her he didn't want a bachelor party, she said it was only because he didn't know anyone who could get him what he wants. "I know you," she said. "You have weird tastes, but I'll plan the perfect party." That's what he was afraid of, Karen's idea of what he really liked.

Karen was the first person he hired when he opened the diner fifteen years ago. She started as a dishwasher, moved onto the grill, then into the front where she waited tables until the previous day manager quit. Over the years, they'd flirted with each other. Once, they'd talked about actually going on a date, but the idea never moved beyond talk. Then, he met Anne Marie.

The stripper swings her breasts back and forth hard enough that they bounce off each other, creating a ricochet effect that sends the men into gales of giggles. Ramsey joins in the laughter but doesn't feel it and stops before he gets started.

The first time he brought Anne Marie to the diner, Karen wrinkled her nose and stared as Anne Marie eased herself into the booth. When Ramsey went to the bathroom, Karen pulled him aside and said, "What do you call that, a muumuu?" He looked over at Anne Marie, who was wearing a loose dress that hung from her shoulders to her knees, hiding her shape. He shrugged and moved past Karen. "Is that really the best you can do?" she called after him. Then, the next time he saw her, she asked, "What are you doing, charity work?" and every day after she made another smartass comment. Until Anne Marie came in wearing a diamond ring. Karen shut up then, but that didn't mean she was done.

The stripper tosses her head to Freddie Mercury's anthem, her hair moving in one clump, as she struts toward Ramsey while his employees cheer her on. She leans over him, her breasts the only thing he can see. "Ready for one last good time?" she says, before pulling his face into her chest. Distantly, he hears his employees chant his name and whistle their encouragement.

When she finally lets him up for air, he holds out two fifties and says, "I'll give you a hundred bucks if you leave." She takes them with her teeth but doesn't move. Instead, she turns her ass to him, a mound of flesh that gives him an erection, and gyrates on his lap. She spins away from him and toward the bar stools where the men yell for her. Hands grab at her ass and breasts and stomach, but she keeps moving, twisting and spinning across the room. The guys sprinkle her with dollar bills, and when she does a split, everyone yells out his name.

Ramsey hears Karen's lighter strike right behind his head, smells the cigarette smoke curling up into the already grease-stained air, toward the fluorescent lights that line the ceiling. He turns to look at her. She stares at him, her lips turned upward in an ugly smile. She says something, but he can't hear her above the din. The men around her laugh, and Ramsey slinks down into his chair. He likes big women, likes the gobs of flesh on Anne Marie's thighs and arms. Likes that he feels dwarfed by her.

Since their engagement, Karen has been leading a revolt among the employees. She's always five or ten minutes late, never enough to fire her but just enough to make her disrespect obvious. She counteracts his smallest decisions—changing Taco Tuesday to Taco Wednesday, which doesn't even make sense, ordering extra ground beef when he said to cut back, giving the new dishwasher a day off when Ramsey already said no. And it's rubbing off—the rest of the staff does what he says, but only halfheartedly, and when they don't like his orders, they run to Karen who changes them.

A few weeks ago, after realizing that sales were down three months in a row, he announced the idea of turning the greasy spoon into a fifties diner, complete with a jukebox and ice cream floats. Actually, it was

Anne Marie's idea. "Picture it: neon lights and bobby socks," she'd said. "Pies under glass lids, thick cut slices topped with vanilla ice cream." And he could picture it, could see half of Brickton sitting at the counter, families bringing their kids in for dinner when the air wasn't saturated with grease and cigarette smoke.

As soon as he shared the idea with his staff, Karen laughed. "That's not what this place is," she said. "We're a dive. Always have been, and you'd be stupid to change it." Since then, she'd been busting his balls about his idea, until he too dismissed it. So, he made a lunch special: two hot dogs, a plate of fries, and a soda for three bucks. He wasn't sure it made much difference, as he hid in his office most of the time now, loathe to deal with Karen or any of his staff.

None of them understands the sex appeal of a big woman, that making love to Anne Marie is like sinking into a giant pillow, his whole body covered in her warm flesh, every bit of him enveloped by her. His employees would be fighting to go home with this stripper if they knew. If he were marrying anyone but Anne Marie, they would have hired a tiny blonde with fake tits. Instead, this woman struts around in her boots, spinning the tassels on her pasties in opposite directions while the men howl. She doesn't know that Ramsey's the only one in the room who appreciates her as she is.

The song winds down, her tassels stop, and she turns to him. "Someone looks a little lonely sitting all by himself," she says. "He's ready for his private dance." Bending her knees, she leans forward and beckons him with a curled finger. Ramsey doesn't move until she grabs his arm and pulls him forward, propelling him toward his office.

"You better enjoy this," Karen whispers as they exit, "cause no one else is." He opens his mouth to say something, but the stripper guides him inside the room and pushes him down into the desk chair, which wheels backward until it hits the edge of his desk. "Give him the works," Karen says and closes the door behind her. There is a roar of voices from the guys out front, but Ramsey tunes them out when the woman puts one leg on either side of his lap, straddling him, her round stomach in his face, the scent of sweat and sex emanating from her skin.

"You don't have to do this," he says, but he's running his hands up her arms, across her stomach.

She doesn't answer, continues to press her body against his. He wonders what the guys outside think, what Anne Marie would think if she saw him.

"This isn't necessary," Ramsey says.

She feels like Anne Marie, but she's harder, muscles hiding under all her fat.

"I respect you," he says and shoves his face into her cleavage, inhaling the scent of sweat.

She steps back and laughs. "I don't care," she says.

He looks up at her face. "You don't have to stay for the whole evening. I can pay you," he says. "I own this place."

"Your friends already paid me."

"They're not my friends," he says. "They're my employees."

"Let's just do this," she says and turns her ass to him again.

He rubs his hands on her thighs but then stops. "Really," he says. "Don't." He pushes her butt away from him.

She looks back at him and sighs. "You're not gonna make this easy, are you?"

"I can make it real easy," he says. "Walk out the door, take a right, and slip out the back."

She sits down in a chair across from him and crosses her legs. Digging inside her boot, she comes up with a pack of cigarettes and a lighter. She takes her time lighting up before looking back at him. "Why would I want to leave?"

"Why wouldn't you?" he asks. She flicks ash onto the floor, but he doesn't say anything.

She shrugs. "I should at least give you your money's worth."

"You did," he says.

"If you think that's all I do, you don't know what you're missing."
She lets more ashes fall to the floor, leaving a burn mark in a carpet
already filled with them. "Besides, we haven't even begun what your
lady friend paid for."

"I don't need to," he says. Ramsey would get up if he could, but with
her chair pulled close to him, legs draped across his thighs, he's trapped.
"Besides," he says, "they're laughing at you." He nods toward the front
of the restaurant where they're replaying "Fat Bottomed Girls." He
hears them shouting but can't make out the words.

"I thought you said you were the boss." More ashes.

"I am."

"You must not be a very good one," she says and takes another
drag. She stares at him, and he looks away.

"I'm a normal-sized guy marrying a fat woman. That means
something."

She drops her cigarette to the floor, unwinds her legs, and grinds
the butt out with her heel. "Means something to who?" she asks.

"I love her," he says. "I think she's beautiful. I think you're beautiful. They don't."

She grabs her breasts, pushes them toward his face. "Those boys
don't know what they're missing."

"They really don't," he says. He can't stop staring at her chest.

She leans toward him, pasties touching his nose. "You want this
dance or not?"

"Yes," he says. He puts his hand on her breast but comes nowhere
near covering all of it.

"You like that?" she asks, and she's back in stripper mode. "You can
kiss them," she says, leaning forward. He licks around the pasties, and
she runs her hand down his chest, rubs the heel of her hand against his

crotch. He groans. She grabs his hair, pulls his head back, and kisses him. Even her lips are big. They envelop him, and Ramsey calls out, but his voice gets lost in the kiss. Then, she's on him, straddling him, her hands opening his pants, pulling him out, her G-string shoved to the side, and he's inside her. She gyrates on his lap, he bucks against her, and too quickly, he comes. She leans back, laughs.

"I'm sorry," he says when he catches his breath. Already, he realizes what he's done, but the stripper is nonplussed. She's standing, cleaning herself up. Ramsey stuffs himself back inside his pants, thinks maybe it wasn't cheating. After all, he didn't do anything, not really. He just reacted.

"Don't be sorry," she says. "That's what you're supposed to do." Then, she sits across from him, her legs draped over him, as though they hadn't had sex only moments before.

"Not really."

"What do you think she paid me for?"

He looks at her, then away, then back at her. She's not lying. "It's Karen's fault," he says.

"What?"

"Nothing," he says, but he's right. Without Karen, he never would have done this, never would have had to go home and lie to Anne Marie. A bit of hatred toward Karen takes root. And he's glad. He needs to hate her for what he's about to do.

"You want to go back out there?" she asks.

"Not yet. I want to enjoy this for a minute."

She takes out her pack of cigarettes and passes it to him. He takes one, lights it, and draws the smoke deep into his lungs. He hasn't smoked in ten years, and it burns but tastes as good as he remembers. He leans back, closes his eyes. "I could make this place nice again," he says. She doesn't respond, but when he opens his eyes, she's looking at him. "Lay new linoleum, get the stools reupholstered, put a new sign out front. Get some high school girls wearing sweater sets and poodle skirts instead of Karen with her sour face. Make it a family diner instead of a greasy spoon."

"What's stopping you?" she asks.

"Nothing," Ramsey says. He takes a drag off his cigarette, blows a smoke ring into the air. "Absolutely nothing."

THE DANCE

———

When Everett appeared in front of Bradley, hair swept back, glasses smudged, Bradley wanted to mess up his own hair, also brushed back. "What's up?" Bradley asked. The gym was draped in streamers, but it looked like someone had toilet papered the basketball court. The bleachers were shoved back, and the teachers had placed little tables all around the dance floor, each one covered in glitter and flowers. No one sat at them. Instead, boys pulled the chairs into groups and bounced a ball back and forth or tried to spit on each other from across the open area.

Bradley scanned the crowd behind Everett's head. The DJ's colored lights shone into his eyes and then moved across people swaying to a Michael Jackson song. It was the same slow song they played at all the dances, where girls snuggled into boys' necks as they moved in tiny circles for four minutes, guys slipping their hands ever lower until the girls dragged them back to their waists. Girls without partners stood in clusters, swaying back and forth, hoping one of the boys would ask them to dance.

"My mom can give you a ride home if you need it," Everett said.

"I'm spending the night at Jeremy's." Bradley kept an eye out for his friends, barely meeting Everett's eye. The two of them had grown up on the same block. At Bradley's end of the street, the houses were old, but people kept their yards trimmed and their windows clean. Moving toward Everett's end of the street, the houses were in progressive stages of disrepair, first with chipped paint or a tire-less car in the yard, then with broken windows and furniture on the porch. The very last house belonged to Everett's family. It had garbage bags in place of some windows and three cars in the front yard, along with an old toilet and claw-foot bathtub. What grass Everett's family had was overgrown with weeds, but most of the yard was packed dirt. Sometimes, Everett's granddad sat on the porch with a can of Stroh's and no shirt.

With their ill-fitting clothes and shoes that split at the sole, Everett's family were sturgeons. There was a divide at school between the sturgeons, the poor and unclean, and everyone else. Bradley always tried to keep Everett out of that group by giving him clothes and forgetting sticks of deodorant at his house when he spent the night. Now that they were in high school, where everyone had more money than either of them, it was all Bradley could do to keep out of the sturgeon group himself. And being a sturgeon in high school meant social suicide—a long four years of mocking and teasing. Even the teachers got in on it, maybe not overtly, but they somehow managed to overlook quite a few of the pranks, even some outright fights. Right now, the only thing that was keeping Bradley on the right side of the divide was his new friend Jeremy, whom he clung to. It wasn't his fault he had to leave Everett behind.

"We're still friends, right?" Everett asked.

"I should go," Bradley said. "Clara's probably looking for me." He liked saying her name, wanted to add "my date" but didn't. Jeremy had set them up. When he and Jeremy had climbed out of his mom's minivan and walked through the door with the girls, everyone had turned to look at them, the only ninth graders to arrive with dates.

"Remember when we used to dance?" Everett said as his face turned a brilliant red. "We still could," he said. "I miss you."

"I don't think that would be a good idea," Bradley said.

This past summer, before coming to Brickton High where the four middle schools in the county consolidated, they had slow-danced to his mom's old records. Everett, who looked so uncoordinated, was a natural on the dance floor. He helped Bradley learn a few moves so he wouldn't make a fool of himself at the monthly high school dances.

They'd stood on Everett's back porch made of worn, uneven boards. "If you can dance here, you can dance anywhere," he said. "You'll look like you're floating."

They wedged giant speakers, the old kind that popped and sputtered, between the sill and the empty window frame. Sometimes, they had to go inside and wiggle the cords in back to make the sound come out. They grabbed a Patsy Cline record from Everett's mom's collection of 45s and set it up so the song would repeat until they turned it off.

"Let's see what you've got," Everett said and put his hands on Bradley's shoulders. Bradley touched Everett's waist with the tips of his fingers, which seemed more intimate than when they wrestled on his floor and the winner had to pull splinters from the loser's back. Bradley moved his feet from side to side, slowly turning Everett in a circle. After a few seconds, Everett stood back and said, "We have a lot of work to do."

When Bradley said, "I'm not that bad," Everett laughed.

They started with a simple box step, but Bradley stepped on Everett's toes for the first two days. Eventually, he memorized where his feet were supposed to go and learned to lead, which was hard. Everett kept saying, "Guide me," but when Bradley tried, Everett would say, "Don't push." Then, Bradley would shove Everett off the porch. When he reached for a hand up, Everett would pull Bradley down with him, where they'd wrestle and punch each other until they were too tired to continue. Then, they'd dance again, covered in dirt.

Once Bradley could go a whole song without messing up, Everett said, "Tomorrow, you're going to show me how much you've learned."

"I only know one step."

"That's all you need."

The following day, Bradley arrived to find Everett wearing dress pants with duct tape covering a hole in the knee. He even wore a tie with his faded button-down shirt. "Was I supposed to dress up?" Bradley asked. He wore denim shorts that were getting too tight, but his mom said that since summer was almost over, he didn't need a new pair.

Everett went inside and put the needle on the record, this time Elton John's "Your Song."

Everett stepped into Bradley's arms. "Pretend I'm your girlfriend," Everett said. Bradley put his hands on Everett's hips. "You wouldn't hold your girlfriend like that," Everett said, and Bradley locked his hands around Everett's waist.

They moved together, no missteps, their breath mingling in the space between them. Everett continued to dance, even once the song was over. Then, the record player's arm made a loud clang, and the song began to repeat. Everett stepped closer and kissed Bradley. His lips were warm and chapped, and Bradley felt a heat in his stomach.

"I'm not like that," he said and let go of Everett's waist.

"Okay."

"I think I have the steps down now," Bradley said, already moving away. "Thanks for teaching me. I should go. I forgot, I told my mom I'd mow the grass today."

"Today?" Everett asked.

Bradley nodded and walked off the porch, through the maze of his backyard with its rusted-out cars and toys that had been dropped and forgotten long ago. "She'll be mad if I don't," Bradley said. He walked home fast, his head down, face hot. It had been his first kiss, but he didn't know if he liked it because of that or because it was from Everett. His guts churned, and he tried to forget it, already distancing himself from his friend even before meeting Jeremy.

"Don't you like me?" Everett asked now, the DJ's colored lights playing across his face.

"Like you how?" Bradley caught Jeremy's eye and watched as he pulled Clara and Melanie over, the kind of girls Bradley's mother said were "asking for trouble," both in dresses too short, bright lipstick slathered across their lips. Jeremy hiked his pants up until you could see his hairless calves and pointed at Everett, whose pants stopped well above his ankles. The girls laughed. Bradley turned red. It wasn't Everett's fault his parents couldn't buy him new pants, but Bradley felt guilty all the same. He used to pass his old clothes off to Everett but hadn't since the end of last school year. When his mom cleaned out his dresser a couple weeks ago, she gave him a bag of clothes for Everett, but Bradley hadn't given them to him, instead hiding them in the bottom of the trashcan in the yard. Everett's shirt was also too small, the sleeves ending above the knobs of his wrists.

"Are we even still friends?"

Before Bradley could answer, Clara appeared behind Everett and smiled at Bradley. Then, she crouched, grabbed the legs of Everett's pants, her red nails vivid against the faded black cloth, and yanked them to the floor.

Bradley stepped back from the guffaws and watched Everett's face turn red as he bent to pull up his pants, tighty whiteys on display. Teachers' flashlight beams cut through the darkness, revealing stains on the back of Everett's underwear and setting off another round of laughter. Mr. Higgins, the principal, put his arm around Everett and started to lead him away from the crowd. Bradley stepped toward them, then stopped. Everett shrugged the principal off. "It was an accident," he said.

The principal looked at him, and Everett met his eye. Mr. Higgins looked away first and scanned the circle of onlookers. His eyes stopped on Jeremy, who was still grinning, but moved past Clara who had now edged her way next to Bradley. She grabbed his hand. He didn't let go but didn't hold on either.

"You're sure?" Mr. Higgins asked.

Everett nodded and turned away. The principal turned off the flashlight but watched as Everett walked across the floor, head held high but not meeting anyone's eye.

"Enjoy that?" Melanie asked. She and Jeremy stood in front of Bradley and Clara, still grinning. Melanie, a tenth grader, was even more popular than Clara, and Jeremy hadn't let go of her hand all night. Mr. Higgins even caught them kissing during a slow song.

"You should leave him alone," Bradley said.

"What?" Jeremy yelled above the music. "We shouldn't pick on your boyfriend?" He said it loud enough that dancers glanced over at them.

"He's not my boyfriend," Bradley said. He looked at Everett who stood on the edge of the dance floor alone.

"What are you doing with a sturgeon?" Clara asked, and Bradley realized that she'd let go of his hand and now stood beside Melanie, the three of them forming a wall in front of him. "You bathe, don't you?" She sniffed the air around him.

"I'm not dirty," he said. "And neither is he."

"Look at him," Clara said. "He's filthy."

Everett was poor, that was obvious, but he showered and kept his clothes clean, even if he couldn't help when they didn't fit.

"I don't hang out with him. Not anymore."

"You sure?" Clara asked.

"Not in a while."

"That's cause you're our friend," Jeremy said and slung his arm over Bradley's shoulder. Bradley let out the breath he hadn't realized he'd been holding. "Right?"

"Yeah." And he was, because Jeremy had taken him in right after he started at Brickton, told the other boys that he was okay, cool even.

The boys had begun inviting him over to their houses for pool parties, and Bradley owed them. He'd never been in any pool but the pee-filled public one he went to with Everett. Clara had only looked at Bradley with his Salvation Army clothes when Jeremy had said he was starting a new trend with old jeans and T-shirts no one else wanted. Jeremy called Bradley retro, and the others believed it. Bradley owed his new friend.

"Prove it," Clara said.

"Prove what?"

"Prove you're not his friend," she said, "and I'll kiss you."

"Okay," he said.

Clara leaned in. "Walk over to him and kick him in the nuts as hard as you can."

"Won't that hurt him?" Bradley asked.

"Duh," Clara said. "He'll crumple and cry for his mommy. It'll be funny."

"No it won't," Bradley said and looked to the others, but they nodded, laughing, Jeremy already cupping his own balls.

He looked over his shoulder and saw Everett still standing on the edge of the dance floor, watching Bradley and the others. He looked back to Jeremy, who smiled and raised his eyebrows. Bradley nodded and walked toward his old friend. Everett looked away as he approached, but Bradley stood in front of him and smiled.

"We're still friends," he said.

"Not really," Everett said and looked over Bradley's shoulder. He turned and saw Jeremy and the girls had inched closer and were watching.

"If you want, we can hang out tomorrow," Bradley said.

Everett looked at him, a half smile on his lips, and shook his head. "You don't have to pretend. It's okay if you don't like me anymore."

Bradley was almost mad at Everett and the way his eyes darted between him and the others.

"Your friends are waiting for you," Everett said and cocked his head toward Jeremy and the girls.

"You're my friend too."

"You're not acting like it."

Bradley realized he was in Everett's space, toes meeting toes, his voice too loud, breath in his friend's face. He stepped back, unclenched his fists, took a deep breath.

"You know they're not really your friends," Everett said. "If you don't do what they tell you, they won't hang out with you anymore."

"How would you know?" Bradley asked. "It's not like they'd even talk to you."

"Then do it," Everett said. "Whatever it is, you can't say no to them."

"No," Bradley said. "I can't."

Everett's hands shook, and Bradley watched the way his friend clenched his eyes shut, opening himself to whatever Bradley had to offer. Their breaths were shallow, almost in unison. Bradley turned back to his new friends who nodded and pretended to kick, their legs cutting through the air. Everett's eyes were still closed, and his lips moved silently. Bradley pulled his leg back, took a deep breath, and stopped. He watched Everett's chest rise and fall, his heart fluttering against his skinny chest, afraid and determined all at once. The way it did when he slept, his heart beating against his ribs. Bradley didn't move.

He glanced down at the floor and back to his old friend. Everett would never have asked him to kick Jeremy in the balls. He looked back to his new friends, Clara making kissing faces at him. Mr. Higgins moved through the dancers, pulling couples apart when they got too close. The DJ's lights flashed and flickered across the gym, the lingering smell of socks and sweat out of place. He looked back to Everett, whose eyes were now open, watching him without expression.

Bradley balled his hands into fists, pulled his foot back, and swung his leg forward as hard as he could. The toe of his shoe mashed into

Everett's crotch. Everett's eyes widened before his legs folded underneath him, and he curled into the fetal position, both hands cupping his balls. Tears ran down his cheeks as he rocked back and forth on the floor.

Bradley watched Everett's agony and couldn't move. Jeremy and the girls crowded in on him, slapping him on the back. Clara wrapped her arms around his neck and planted a kiss on his mouth, but Bradley didn't return it. His mouth remained slack, his eyes on Everett who lay still. Mr. Higgins came forward, knelt beside him, and said something, but Everett didn't respond. Instead, he turned his head to the side and vomited.

Students backed up, whispering, their eyes darting between Bradley and Everett. Clara took hold of Bradley's hand and tried to pull him away, but Bradley was rooted to the floor, paralyzed. He shook off Clara's hand, and she backed away, joining the others. A circle of students had formed around Everett, Mr. Higgins, and Bradley. He stared at his friend's prone body, then at the group. They stared back at him.

Bradley pushed his way through the circle. Once outside the group that surrounded Everett, he ran. Across the gym, out the double doors, and into the night. He stopped at the edge of the road and took a gulp of air, then another. There were no cars out, no noise, a few dimly lit windows in the houses that lined the road but no movement from within. The air was cool, a hint of fall's arrival. Bradley turned at a sound behind him, but it was only a raccoon skittering across the pavement. No one had followed him outside. No one stood at the doors looking out. He was alone. He sat on the curb and waited for someone to claim him.

THE TATTOO

"How could I not have seen it?" Jack leaned forward and stared at Martha's right ear, lifting her sand-colored hair to follow the straight line across the back of her head. It never got thicker than it was at the edge of her hairline, but when he reached the middle of her skull, it blossomed into an eyeball complete with veins and dilated pupil. Even without a socket, the eye looked like it was bulging out of the middle of her head. The tattoo thinned into a line again that ran from each side of the eyeball, ending at the crease where scalp and ear meet, traversing the back of her head.

"The new girl used clippers instead of scissors, so my hair's too short."

He gripped the steering wheel, even though they were still idling in the parking lot of their apartment complex. "So you wore a hat," he said and dropped the pink ball cap in her lap. "Were you planning on sleeping in it too?"

"Our reservation's for six, right?" she asked.

"You have a tattoo on your head. Who cares about dinner?"

Jack looked at her, but Martha had pulled down the sun visor and stared into the mirror, arranging the hat again.

"It's just ink, not a tattoo."

"What's the difference?"

"A tattoo means something."

"You hid it from me. Doesn't that make it mean something?"

"Ronald and Cam will worry," she said. She pulled a tube of lipstick from her purse and turned back to the mirror.

"Look at me," he said, but she applied the lipstick, rubbed her lips together, and used her nail to scrape the bits that had bled into the skin around her mouth. He sighed. "Why did you get it?"

"It's rude to invite them out and then be late. We're celebrating."

It was Ronald and Cam's engagement party, Jack's and Martha's too if she said yes. The maître d' was in on it—his job was to make sure Martha's dessert plate had a ring in the middle. The moment she looked at it would be Jack's cue to get on his knee.

First, Jack needed to learn about the tattoo. "Why on your head?" he asked.

"I haven't talked to Cam since she said yes."

"Why is it an eye?"

"Traffic's getting worse." Martha gestured to Patterson Drive, where lines of cars were forming. It was almost six, and people who commuted into Pittsburgh were trying to get home. "I don't want to make them wait."

Their car crawled along with the others, but Jack drove in silence. He watched the buildings that crowded closer to the road as each block became more rundown than the one before. This area used to be the arts district, before the arts died out and it became the poverty district. Now, instead of cafés and studios, pawnshops and neon-lit bail bond companies lined the road.

Jack knew almost nothing about Martha's past, and that was by design. When they'd met, he was new to Pittsburgh from Brickton, West Virginia, and he was busy erasing his country twang and quitting dipping snuff. She was in the process of erasing the hippie artist she'd been in her twenties, when she, Ronald, and Cam had sold handmade paintings on a street corner a couple blocks from where the restaurant was now.

Neither of them brought up who they used to be or why they'd refashioned themselves. They agreed that it was more important to focus on the present. Actually, Martha said that and he'd agreed. He'd changed because he wanted a pretty girl to like him. Martha seemed to have a deeper reason, but he'd never asked and she'd never shared. Cam and Ronald kept their mouths shut too, and though Jack always suspected there was something he didn't know, he'd never asked.

Now, he tried to picture the Martha who would let someone take a tattoo gun to the back of her head, but he didn't know that person. "You had to shave your head," he said.

She didn't answer, so he glanced at her, but she was looking out the window. "They're already here," she said, "standing outside."

Jack pulled into the lot of Provence Market, their favorite restaurant. Before he shifted into park, Martha was already out of the car and talking to Cam and Ronald.

There had once been a flea market in the lot where the restaurant sat, but it still had the charm of an older building, complete with ivy growing on the bars over the windows. The parking lot had never been repaved, the old vendor lines still visible under the newer parking spaces.

Cam and Ronald both grinned as Jack stepped forward. He smiled back but couldn't work up the same enthusiasm for tonight that he'd had earlier. He looked at Cam, whose past was still visible in the eight piercings in each ear and the scars in her nose and eyebrow from piercings grown over. Ronald had cleaned up more easily, and between his shining bald head and creased khakis, there were no visible traces of his artist past. "Were you there when Martha got her tattoo?" he asked.

"You're not even going to congratulate them?" Martha asked before Ronald or Cam could answer.

Jack shook Ronald's hand. "How's it feel?" he asked.

"The same," Ronald and Cam said at almost the same moment. That was no surprise. Their wedding felt like an afterthought, as though they'd been married for years and were just now getting around to having the requisite celebration.

Jack and Ronald followed the women inside Provence Market, where the maître d' led them to their table, a white cloth draped over his forearm, as though this were a better restaurant in a nicer part of town. He smiled, his lips full and wet.

They'd barely sat when Jack said, "Ronald, you knew about Martha's tattoo, right?"

"Do we have to do this now?" Martha asked.

"I'd forgotten about those tattoos," Ronald said. "I shaved her head, and Cam shaved Donnie's in the kitchen of our old apartment. We should've done it in the bathroom. We found hair in our food for months."

"Donnie?" Jack asked.

"They each got one," Cam said. "Then, they'd stand shoulder to shoulder, so it looked like they were watching us with those bulging eyes."

Ronald and Cam laughed, and Jack wondered that he'd never heard this story before. He looked over at Martha who had buried her face in the menu, though none of them had opened a menu here in over a year.

"Who's Donnie?" he asked.

Martha looked up and said, "We're here to celebrate. Let's talk about something else." Her face was pale, and sweat beaded on her forehead.

"No way," Cam said. "Ronald proposed here, like we all knew he would, and there's not much more to say. Besides, this is great. I haven't thought about those tattoos in forever. Can I see yours?"

Jack took Martha's head in his hands and tilted it around toward Cam. Martha's face was inches from his, but she closed her eyes. "I can't do this," she said.

Cam leaned forward. "Look," Jack said and traced the tattoo with his finger. They followed the line until it blossomed into an eyeball. Cam reached out to touch it.

Before they could follow it all the way to her other ear, Martha turned her head and said, "I think we all get the picture." Her face was red, and Jack wasn't sure if she was embarrassed or angry, maybe both.

The waiter stopped by to take their orders. He smiled at them, and Jack noticed that most of the waiters had glanced at their table more than once, some giving him a thumbs up when Martha's back was turned. He kept silent and looked away. Martha stared at her menu.

Jack, Cam, and Ronald ordered steaks as usual. They waited for Martha to ask for hers, but she said, "I'll have the roasted duckling."

"Do you even like duck?" Jack asked when their waiter was gone.

"Would I order it if I didn't?" Martha asked, and Jack blushed.

"Apparently there's a lot I don't know about you," he said.

There was a moment of silence. Then, "You didn't know about the tattoo?" Cam asked.

"I just saw it today," he said. "I only heard about Donnie today. I still don't know who he is."

"Was," Ronald said.

Jack looked over at Martha, but she stared down at the table. "Who was he, then?" he asked.

"Her boyfriend," Cam said.

"Our friend," Ronald added.

A gloom descended over their table.

"He died," Cam said.

"He was buying pills for us," Ronald said. "Someone stabbed him. They never caught the guy who did it."

Jack felt like they were sitting at one table, he at another.

"We cleaned up then," Cam said. "For Donnie."

It made sense. When he first moved to Pittsburgh and decided he had to have Martha, Jack felt like he was trying on a whole new person, his clothes still creased from the store, his accent popping out at odd moments, refusing to disappear completely. One reason he'd liked Martha was because she wasn't quite comfortable in her skin either. He loved the way she ran her fingers through her hair, as though she weren't sure where it had come from. That he fit into their group like they'd been waiting for him. He realized now that it was because they had been. He was only a replacement.

"It's an ugly tattoo," he said.

"It's none of your business," Martha said and slammed the heel of her hand on the table. Jack's glass fell and hit his plate, cracking down the side. He watched the wine soak into the tablecloth, heard the conversations at the other tables fall silent. Cam jumped up and started blotting the mess, but it ran across the table and over the side. Jack felt the liquid pool in his lap and watched as his khakis turned red.

The maître d' scrambled to the table and began to apologize, laying towels over the mess and pressing one into Jack's hand. Jack looked up at him and said, "I don't think I want dessert after all." Apparently all one of the other waiters heard was the word dessert, because he rushed over and placed a plate with a silver cover in the middle of the table. "Ta-da!" he said and revealed the ring. He and the maître d' stood back. The other waiters stopped what they were doing and looked over at their table. Patrons began to clap.

Jack looked at his friends. Martha looked at the ring. Cam and

Ronald didn't seem to know what to do. Their eyes moved from Martha to the ring to Jack. None of them moved. The guests stopped clapping and began talking too fast and too loud, while waiters hurried to refill water glasses.

Jack stood and reached for the cover. He placed it on the ring, turned to Martha, said, "Let's start over."

She looked at him. "How?"

He paused, cleared his throat, and said in his best Brickton accent, "I'm Jack, I love fishing, I hate shirts with collars, and I want to know everything about you."

GRIEF

——

When I walked through the front door, my old man lay on the couch, cradling a dog that wore my mom's yellow nightgown. Its nails were painted a bright pink, the same color Mom always wore. The dog shook its head, and there was makeup smeared across its face. The scent of perfume wafted across the room.

"Dad?" I said. He was asleep, his arms curled around the dog. He looked old, more haggard than the last time I'd seen him. His face was slack, the lines around his mouth deeper, his cheeks etched with crevices that spider-webbed out from the corners of his eyes. It was as though mom's death had leached all the flesh from his bones. One week since her burial and already he looked frail, like he would disappear right in front of me.

He began to stir, stretching and scratching the dog behind its ears, muttering to it. Then, he saw me and jumped. He stood, the dog behind him, as though he could hide what he'd been doing. "You shouldn't be here," he said. His voice shook. It was four in the afternoon, but he wore pajamas and a bathrobe.

I stood in the middle of the room, nothing to say.

The dog jumped down from the couch and stretched, front legs forward, its ass up in the air. Then it circled the room, Mom's night-gown trailing behind it. Every few steps, it reached around and tried to bite the gown off. The retriever's fur was the same shade of blonde my mom's hair had been.

My dad had never liked dogs unless they lived outdoors and chased squirrels or rabbits during hunting season, and now this one wandered freely around the room. I didn't even know he'd gotten it. When I was a boy, I'd begged him for a dog, but Dad always said I wouldn't take care of it or that we weren't pet people or that I could have one once I got a job and paid for it myself or any other excuse he could think of to make sure no dog ever showed up on our front stoop. Once, a stray beagle came around the house, and I fed it until it disappeared. Dad told me it had run off, but I found it in the woods a few days later, cold and dead, a bullet hole in its head. I never asked for a dog again. That was thirty years ago, and even when I got my own place, I didn't consider adopting one.

"What's going on?" I asked.

"Just taking an afternoon nap," he said and smiled as though there weren't a dog dressed in my mom's clothes right behind him. "What's up with you?"

"It's a rabbit dog?" Anger crept into my voice.

"Just a pet." He shrugged. "Don't you have to work today?"

"What do you think you're doing?" I yelled it, the anger erupting from my mouth.

"Nothing wrong with a man having a dog in his old age, is there?" He looked small. He reached down and smoothed the dog's coat with his palm.

"Yes," I said. "There is. For you, anyway."

My face was turning red. When I got really mad, the color crept up my cheeks to my forehead, all the way to my bald spot.

"It's okay, Bess," he cooed to the dog. "Tim doesn't get it."

"You don't name a fucking dog after your fucking wife," I said. Mom's body wasn't even cold yet. My hands shook. I balled them into fists, took a step forward and then back. I'd never hit my dad before, had only really wanted to a few times when I was a teenager and he was being an ass, but it took everything in me to turn away from him and walk to the front door.

"I won't let you do this," I said, spittle flying from my mouth.

Dad didn't say a word. He stood in the middle of the living room, his hand buried in the scruff of the dog's neck. The dog lifted its back leg, scratching at the nightgown. I shook my head and slammed the door behind me.

I drove the five miles to my house, slowed as I came near, but then sped up again. I knew what I'd find inside: silence, half-empty rooms, and mismatched furniture I'd gotten second-hand when I bought the house fifteen years ago. For the past week, I'd been hiding out there, watching television, eating TV dinners, and drinking cans of Bud. I couldn't return to that.

Before, I'd have gone to Mom and Dad's house. Most days, I went there after work and ate dinner with them. It was warm, inviting, smelling of baking bread and the smoke from Mom's ever-present Salem. Later, we'd watch Jeopardy together, calling out answers when we knew them, commenting on how we'd all kick butt at the first round of the game and fall apart in the second. Then, if I didn't feel like going to my own house, I'd sleep in my childhood bedroom. There were weeks when I spent only one night at my own house, and sometimes I wondered why I kept it. But now, with Dad's new houseguest, I was glad I had it, even if I didn't want to go there.

I wondered what all he did with that dog. It wore my mom's clothes, it smelled like her, but that had to be all. My dad might be sick, but he wasn't that sick, right? I pulled up in front of the Elks and pushed the thought away. My dad was lonely. That's all.

The Elks was in a cinder-block building, rebuilt after the original burned in a grease fire that got out of control. The parking lot was full of trucks I recognized. They belonged to guys who spent most of their days perched on bar stools sipping beer and playing the poker machines, a few others who sat in the back room and played pinochle for hours every day. I didn't feel like talking to any of them, but I didn't know where else to go—the place I'd always gone to when I was out of sorts had been taken over by a demented old man and his dog.

I didn't realize until Mom got really sick, but Dad was mostly silent during my visits. He sat in the living room napping or watching TV while Mom and I talked over plates of food. Once she was bedridden, I'd watch TV with Dad for a few minutes before visiting Mom in her room, talking to her if she was awake or holding her hand while she slept. Dad and I rarely talked, except to discuss how Mom was doing. When she died, we made funeral plans. After, on the ride home from the cemetery, we were quiet. Even when he got out of my truck, we had nothing to say, just nodded, and I watched him walk inside. I'd called once, but that was awkward too. Mom had been the glue that held us together.

I stepped out of the truck and hitched up my pants. Inside, the air was smoky, the windows covered in dark curtains, the smell of deep fryer grease in the air. I took a seat at the end of the bar, away from the others who'd congregated at a table across the room.

"A Bud," I told Carla, the bartender. She'd been working there as long as I could remember, her frizzy gray hair and smoke-ravaged voice a fixture in the bar. She set her cigarette in the ashtray and pulled a beer from the tap.

"How you doing, Tim?" she asked and put the glass in front of me. "How about your dad?"

"We're doing okay," I said and smiled. "One day at a time."

Until that moment, I'd assumed Dad had been in the Elks since the funeral. He was one of the guys who spent his days playing pinochle. I didn't ask Carla, as I didn't want her to confirm what I knew: that Dad had spent the past week cuddling his new pet.

She put her hand on mine. "We're thinking of you two."

I nodded, my throat tight. Dad had been a member of the Elks Club since he turned eighteen, and he brought me in on my twenty-first birthday. We'd known the people in here for years. I could name all of them, went to high school with some, others were my dad's friends. Most of them had come to Mom's showing, and those who hadn't sent flowers. The guys at the table were eyeing me, talking softly. I didn't want them to ask me how I was, how my dad was. I didn't want to be here. I chugged my beer in two gulps, but by the time I set my empty glass on the bar, Dan Morgan was already sitting on the stool beside me.

"You got our flowers?" he asked. "We were still in Florida."

I nodded.

"We were sorry to hear about your mom," he said and squeezed my shoulder.

I was close to crying, tears perched on my lower lids, but I swallowed the sob and said, "Thanks, Dan. That means a lot, to my dad too."

"You take care of that old man of yours," he said and stood. "Tell him to come and see us. First beer's on me."

"I'll do my best." Before he made it back to his seat, I laid a five on the bar and was already out the door, shading my eyes in the sudden sunlight. I sat behind the wheel of my truck, waiting. My hands shook, and my eyes blurred with tears. I couldn't see the dashboard, never mind the road. Another truck pulled into the lot, and the driver honked. "Tim," he called. It was one of my dad's friends. I waved and shifted into reverse, wiping the tears from my eyes. "Hold up a minute," he said and got out of his truck. I hit the gas, pulling onto the road while he walked toward me.

I could barely see as I drove, but I'd taken the route enough times that I knew it from memory. By the time I made it back to my house, my eyes had cleared, but my breathing was ragged. I parked in the dirt clearing in front of my little house and gulped air. I stepped out of the truck, but my legs were rubbery. I put my head down on the hood and waited for the feeling to pass.

I wasn't sure the last time I'd eaten. The day before, maybe. At some point, I'd run out of TV dinners and ignored the ache in my gut. No wonder I felt like shit. I went inside and opened the fridge, but I hadn't been to the store in who knows how long. Mom used to send me home with so many leftovers I almost never shopped for myself. All I had was mustard, ketchup, some bologna, and I didn't know how old it was. The rest of the shelves were empty. The cupboards were just as bare, a box of stale crackers that I hadn't closed completely and a couple cans of green beans. I slammed the door, grabbed my keys, and walked back outside.

I meant to get in my truck and go to the store, but instead, I doubled over and started bawling. Right in the middle of my front yard. I sobbed like I hadn't the morning Dad called to tell me Mom had died during the night, the way I hadn't at the mass they'd said at the funeral, or when they'd lowered her casket into the ground. I howled like a little kid. Then, once all that sadness found its way out of me, I was left with a kind of anger I'd never felt before. I was mad at my dad and his stupid dog, at my mom for dying, at God for taking her. I was mad at the world for taking all my safe places.

"Goddammit," I said and kicked the truck's bumper. "Stupid fucking son of a bitch." I kicked the bumper again and again, cursing at the top of my lungs, tears and snot running down my face. I kicked until the fiberglass buckled and splintered, and I kept on kicking until I fell backward. I lay on the ground and howled. I thought of my father sitting at his house with only that stupid dog to hold onto while he cried, and it made me blubber even more. I thought of my mom and the way she told me once, "It doesn't matter that you're grown. I'm your mom, and it's my job to take care of you." That finally made the tears stop flowing. I lay on the ground, staring up at the sky that was steadily darkening, the air turning cold, and realized that it was my job to take care of my dad and myself now. He and the dog were my responsibility. I stood, my whole body sore. None of my neighbors was outside, but you could bet a few of them had been watching from behind their curtains. I walked back to the house.

I stood in the shower until the hot water tank ran cold. Then, I pulled on a pair of boxers, lay on my bed, and slept like the dead. I didn't dream. I didn't pull the covers out from under me. I didn't even roll over. It was the best night's sleep I'd had since before Mom was diagnosed.

The next morning, I woke with the sunrise. I opened my eyes and knew what I had to do. I gathered a bunch of boxes and threw them in the back of the truck to take over to Dad's. The dog wasn't taking the nightgown. I'd bought that for Mom when she first got sick. The dog wasn't taking any of her other clothes either. I would pack them all up and take them with me. If Dad wanted a dog, he could treat it like the mutt it was.

I stomped my feet and called out as I walked in his house. I didn't want to surprise him again. Still, I stood in the entryway until he acknowledged me. "I have coffee." I held two Styrofoam cups from the Pantry Store. Dad made a pot of coffee every morning, and it tasted better than the cheap stuff you got from the store, but it felt weird to show up with nothing. Of course, the whole thing was odd—I didn't even know the house without Mom. It didn't smell the same anymore. It stunk of old man and of sickness and dying. Just a few weeks ago, it still smelled like baking bread and spices.

Dad was dressed, which was already better than yesterday. The dog approached me and growled low in its throat, but Dad clapped his hands and said, "It's okay, Bess. You know Tim."

Then, as though it really did know me, the dog approached and sniffed at my crotch before putting its front paws on my chest and keening to be petted. The nightgown trailed to the ground. The dog's nails were still painted, and it smelled like Mom's perfume. "Down," I said and removed its paws.

"We need to talk." I handed Dad the cup of coffee.

He took a sip, winced, and waved for me to follow him into the kitchen. There, he took my coffee too and dumped them both down the sink. He handed me a fresh cup from his pot. It already had extra milk in it. "Sugar?" I asked.

He nodded.

"You knew I'd come."

"After yesterday," he said and trailed off.

He sat at the table, and the dog planted itself between his legs. He reached his hand out automatically and buried it in the dog's fur.

"I was surprised," I said but didn't know how to continue.

He nodded but didn't look at me. I sat in the chair across from him, the same one I'd sat in my whole life.

He cleared his throat. "Bess," he started again. "The dog—"

"It's not good," I said.

"The house is empty," he said.

"I miss her too."

He nodded, met my eyes. I stared back into his.

"Sometimes, it gets lonely," I said. There were other things I wanted to say, questions to ask, but I couldn't get them out. All the things I'd prepared were gone.

"Exactly." He clapped his hand on my shoulder and stood.

I watched as he refilled his own cup of coffee and then nodded at mine. I held out my nearly full mug, and he topped it off.

"That stuff from the Pantry Store is shit," he said.

"I know."

He sat across from me again. I could see him relaxing into normalcy, but I had to go on. "But Bess?" I said. "You had to give her Mom's name too?"

"What's wrong with that?" he asked. "I thought your mom would like it."

"It's a dog," I said. "That's an insult to Mom's memory."

"The hell you say."

"I think this has gone far enough," I said.

"What?"

"The dog, Mom's clothes," I said. I tried to choose my next words carefully. "It's unhealthy. I should have stopped in sooner. I should have been taking better care of you."

His face turned red, all the way up to his bald spot. I got that from him. "You think that's your job?"

"I didn't mean—"

"You damn well did," he said. "And I'm fine. You don't need to worry yourself about that."

I stood, flustered. I'd started off wrong. "I'm donating Mom's clothes," I said. "I brought boxes."

He stood and took a step toward me, his hands balled into fists.

"Your dog can't wear her clothes. I won't allow it." I put my coffee down and walked outside. I breathed in the cool morning air. I could let him keep an outfit or two, but not the nightgown. I grabbed a few boxes from the truck, but when I turned around, Dad was in my face.

"You won't allow me?" he said. Then, he hit me, reached back and punched me. I staggered backward. Blood dripped on my fingers, and the pain exploded in my face. My nose was broken. I looked at him, and Dad said, "I didn't mean—" I didn't let him finish. Instead, I charged him and threw my shoulder into his chest, tackling him. We went sprawling across the yard, and I got on top of him and threw punches anywhere they'd land—his mouth, his ear, his neck. At first, Dad let me. He covered his face but didn't try to fight back. The dog circled us, barking and growling, but didn't approach.

I glanced up, and the damn thing looked crazy, dragging Mom's nightgown through the grass. While I was distracted, Dad reached up and threw me off of him. He'd always been bigger than me, and he might look frail, but he was still strong. I realized how strong when I hit the ground, my breath gone.

"Who the hell do you think you are?" he yelled. He stood above me, his face already bloody and swollen from the blows I'd landed. There were tears in his eyes too, the first I'd ever seen. They slid down his cheeks, but he didn't wipe them away.

His dog ran to him and growled at me, and Dad's hand automatically found the ruff of her neck. He squatted beside her and whispered in her ear while I caught my breath. I had to admit they looked almost sweet. Sick and twisted, but sweet too. My nose still bled, and tears leaked from my eyes. Dad sat on the lawn and shook his head at me. "That's no way to talk to your dad."

"What'd you expect?" I asked and pinched the bridge of my nose.

He kneaded the dog's fur and looked across the yard. "What'd you do to your truck?"

"Nothing," I said.

"That's not nothing." He nodded toward the mangled bumper.

"It pissed me off," I said.

"Really?" There was a hint of a smile on his lips. "What'd it do, try to wear your mom's clothes?"

When I looked at him, his smile was wide. I looked at the dog— the nightgown was covered in mud, its tongue lolled out the side of its mouth. And my dad's arm was slung around its neck. I realized that he'd be okay. He and that damn dog would be fine. He looked at me, raised his eyebrows, and I couldn't hold it in. First, it was just a little chuckle; then I couldn't stop myself. I fell backward on the grass laughing. I looked over, and my dad was laughing too. For a few minutes there, anyone who drove by would think we were crazy, two grown men rolling on the ground while a golden retriever in a yellow nightgown watched.

THE DOLLAR GENERAL

———

Mom wants to yell; I can see it. Her face changes color, and she takes a deep breath. Her lips move, and I know she's counting to ten, so I say, "Sorry," real quiet. I look at the mess on the floor: GI Joe boxes stacked into dollhouse walls with empty Bratz doll boxes scattered everywhere. The dolls are piled in a heap on top of a baby car, and their evening dresses and disco shorts are strewn across the floor. "I can put it back," I say, but she's looking at my Easter outfit. A black streak down the front of my white shirt, maybe from climbing up the display to reach the clothes. The knees of my pink pants are brown. I hide my hands in my pockets. The dirt has even made its way under my nails.

We're going to Mrs. Taylor's for dessert. My mom cleans her house. She won't let me go, not like this. "We can get something else," I say. "They sell clothes here." Mom's eyes are fixed on my outfit.

Then, quiet, like a whisper but using her real voice, she says, "Do you think I'm made of money?"

We were at the Dollar General to get cleaning supplies, and Mom said I could look at the Bratz dolls while she shopped. They're better than Barbie, because they have lots of makeup, crimped hair, and punk rock clothes. I grabbed a box from the shelf and pulled the cardboard tab out of the slot, peering down at the top of the doll's head. She had a Mohawk. I slid her out of the box and saw the yellow, pink, and purple stripes in her hair. The twisty-ties around her arms, legs, and waist pinned her to the cardboard insert, and I untied those too.

My Brat walked along the shelf, but she needed someone to play with, so I opened another box and pulled a dark-haired doll out. She was a Bratz doll too, but her box said Claudia. They walked together along the shelf, and my Brat said, "Go get me some clothes. I don't like this outfit," so Claudia climbed the shelves. I'm not sure why the store has Bratz dolls and Barbie clothes, but they do, so she pulled a green dress and leopard print pants from the display. The clothes are encased in plastic fronts glued to cardboard backs, so I helped Claudia open them. I looked around before I stood and threw the packaging between the shelves. "What's taking so long?" my Brat yelled, so Claudia grabbed the outfits from me and climbed down to the floor. I had to rip the Barbie pants at the ankle to get them on the Brat, but she liked them. Once she got dressed, she wanted a car, so Claudia crawled up the shelves until she found one in the baby section. While they sat on top of the car, I took more boxes from the shelves to build them a house. I was putting the finishing touches on it when Mom walked up.

"Well?" she says, but I know whatever I say will be wrong. I turn away, but my elbow hits the GI Joe boxes, and they tumble to the floor. I bend down and start picking them up.

I keep my head down and throw the Bratz boxes back on the shelf any which way. There's a loud crack. I jump when Mom's basket hits the floor. She doesn't say anything else, but she looks even paler than usual. It might be the fluorescent lights, but her lips are trembling too. I see that glassy look in her eyes, the one she always has when she says she's too tired to get out of bed that day and I have to eat cereal for all my meals because I'm too little to use the stove. Without looking at me, she turns, walks down the aisle, and around the corner.

"Mom?" I call, but she doesn't answer. I grab the rest of the boxes and pile them on the bottom shelf. I need to catch her. I don't see the open boxes for the Bratz dolls, so I try to shove them between the display cases, but they're too big. I slip them behind the My Little Ponies and then cram the Barbie clothes between the displays. I run toward the front of the store.

Mom's gone.

I go to the aisle with the cleaning supplies. She might have forgotten something and gone to get it while I put up the toys. I like to place things in neat rows like Mom does when she cleans houses.

It's my job to hold the funnel when she pours the generic cleaners into the brand name bottles. I asked her once if it's lying to do that, but she said that because the ladies don't know the difference, it's fine. I don't know whether to believe her, because she whips me even if I tell a little lie.

I run to the back of the store and check the bathrooms before I continue to the shoes and clothes. Maybe she's hiding in a display; maybe she's just trying to scare me. I bend down to peek under a rack of polyester pants, looking for her feet. When I stand up, one of the women who works there is staring at me.

She squats, her hands on her knees, her face close up to mine. "Where's your mom, hon?"

She's our neighbor. Her nose is full of pockmarks, and her yellow shirt matches the sign outside. Her bangs are frizzy. She smiles at me with horsey teeth. She has a swing set in her yard. It's old and rusty, but I sit on it sometimes on Mom's bad days. "She went to the grocery store." I point to the far wall and put on the smile I use when she comes to the window and looks at me on her swing. "I thought I could catch her before she left, but I guess I'll just walk over there."

The woman stands up to her full height and looks around. "Why were you looking in the racks?"

"I saw a bug," I say. "A big one." The woman looks at the floor, and I know she's seen them too. "I should go," I say, and she nods and turns away.

I return to the toy aisle in case Mom's there, but it's empty. I head toward the front of the store. The lady's back is to me, and she's talking to a younger woman who works there, but I hear her say, "—the kid a break. Her mom wanders around the neighborhood in her nightgown," and I know she's talking about my mom. But Mom only did that once, and it was because she couldn't find me.

My mouth waters. I realize I'm hungry, that we're supposed to be at Mrs. Taylor's right now, and I should be eating. I grab a Hershey bar off the display and walk to the door real fast. My neighbor is staring at me. Outside, I give her the finger and then run inside Shop 'N Save. But Mom isn't here. Or if she is, I won't find her. There are too many people. I run back out the door.

Mom parked in the back of the lot, and I make my way there, weaving between the cars so no one sees me. I cram the candy bar in my mouth and chew. I jump over the cracks in the lot but stomp in the puddles left from last night's storm. My pants stick to my legs, and my arms are speckled with mud. When I get to her spot, there's just an empty shopping cart. The blue car with the white hood is gone. I run two rows over and then back in case I was thinking of the last time we came to the Dollar General, but it's all pickup trucks. I see a blue car farther down the row and run to it, but it's too new to be Mom's.

I move between the cars, kicking dandelions that poke up in the cracks of asphalt, too tired now to jump in the puddles. My legs hurt, and my head's starting to ache. My mouth is sticky from the chocolate, and I want a big cup of Kool-Aid with lots of ice. It's hot. Sweat slides down my neck and into my T-shirt. I wipe it away, but my whole back is wet. I return to Mom's empty space and sit beside the cart. I can see everything from here, so I'll stand if Mom's car comes back.

I look up each time a car enters the lot. The sun makes its way across the sky, and the shade that covers me disappears. I wonder if she went to Mrs. Taylor's without me, if she'll bring me a piece of angel food cake, or maybe some turkey. Mom has to come back. When she does, I'll get in the car, and we'll act like nothing ever happened.

CONTROLLED FALL

—

Nathan shoved me, and I said, "Let go," but Marney moved too slowly, and both of us ended up in a heap on the living room floor. "Faster," I told her, "or we'll both get hurt."

"I'm sorry," she said and stood.

"Don't be sorry," I said. "Do it right."

Then Nathan shoved me from behind, and Marney stepped away. I loosened my limbs, let myself fall, and landed unhurt.

"Good," I said. "Again."

"Don't forget to protect your neck," Nathan said. "You're safe here, but what if you're in public?"

We'd thrown yoga mats around my living room and pushed the furniture to the walls, creating a place for me to practice, but Nathan was right. The last time I'd fallen, I was at the grocery store and had crashed into a shelf on my way down. I'd hit the floor and held my hands over my head as cans of tomatoes rained down on me. I'd left with a swollen knee and can-sized bruises forming all over my body. I'd hired Marney a week later. She served as my companion, someone to help me traverse this new world until I could do it alone.

"Like this," Nathan said and showed something to Marney. I closed my eyes and waited, not that it made much difference now whether my eyes were opened or closed. My world had reduced itself to faint outlines, blurred movement, and large swathes of color, the loss both faster and more startling than my doctors had expected. First the problem was confined to books, then moved on to television, until people and objects began to lose their sharp lines, and I had to differentiate by color alone. Now, even colors had begun to fade.

Marney grabbed my arm, and I pulled away. "Not like that," I said. "I'm not a cripple. I'm blind."

I held out my hand, and she put it in the crook of her elbow, like I'd shown her. I didn't hear Nathan's footsteps and wasn't ready when he grabbed my ankle. I toppled to the floor without letting go of Marney, forcing her to come with me.

"That's not fair," I said, rubbing my ankle.

"What isn't?" Nathan asked.

"I didn't hear you that time."

"You wouldn't hear anything in a real fall," Marney said.

"Don't you think I know that?" I said. "I'm sixty years old. It only takes one wrong landing to crack a hip, and I don't want it to happen when someone's throwing me on the floor."

"I'm not throwing you," Nathan said. "I'm helping you."

Marney was sniffling. "What are you crying about?" I asked and wondered again why I hadn't hired someone with experience, someone who was more than a year out of high school.

"I'm not crying," Marney said, but her voice gave her away.

At least she wasn't sobbing, which she'd done the day I hired her, when I asked her to walk more softly through my house. Marney was a heavy girl, and her footsteps made the floor vibrate. I had to remind myself that she was young, that I had done her mom a favor by hiring her. Marney wasn't the brightest girl, but she could listen to directions, which was all I needed.

"Nathan," I said, "can we be finished for the day?"

"You need to get this, Agnes," he said. I could hear the fatigue in his voice. This was the third week we'd practiced falling, and he said we needed to move on to controlling other aspects of my life. I didn't think he had anything to show me beyond falling, going limp, letting myself hit the floor with a dull thud. My body was always covered in bruises now, but there were no worse injuries. I'd never realized how many things stuck out of walls and off furniture.

Beyond that, most of what Nathan said was about how to arrange food on the stove and how to put it on the plate so that it was the same every time. How to rearrange my cabinets and the glory of extra large buttons. Like I was a child.

"We'll practice," I said. "Won't we, Marney?"

"Yes," she said. "By next week, we'll have it down."

Whatever we said must have worked, because Nathan left. I ran my hand along the wall until I reached my bedroom. There, I turned on the radio and ignored Marney's grunts as she pushed the living room furniture back into place.

***

"I checked out some books from the library," Marney said before setting my plate on the table. "They said it's harder to go blind than to be born that way. Your body will automatically adjust to having only four senses when you're a baby. But you'll have to train yourself."

"You sound like Nathan," I said, but she ignored me.

"I thought we could practice a technique with supper. I won't tell you what we're eating, just set it in front of you. Then, you guess."

Marney sounded pleased with herself, as though she were the first person to try this.

"No," I said.

"What?"

"I've done this before. It doesn't help. Believe me. I can't tell chicken from turkey. I don't know apple from grape juice. And I won't do it again."

Marney squatted. "Please," she said, "just once. And I won't bother you again."

The begging in her voice was clear, that she had finally found something she could do right besides clean the house. The day before, she'd burned toast, and the coffee had grounds in it. Before that, she brought Mabel Simms home from the grocery store with her. I locked myself in the bathroom and wouldn't come out until Marney sent her away.

"I told you, no visitors," I'd said. It was the only rule I'd given her. When I first noticed my sight was deteriorating, I pretended I wasn't paying attention when I missed a detail. I went to a doctor who told me that laser surgery was the only thing that would stop the vessels in my eyes from leaking. It was simple, he said. Blast the blood vessels that were already bad and a few more minor surgeries when and if others acted up. During the surgery, that same doctor had been too liberal with the laser. I woke up with half the eyesight I'd had beforehand, and the rest of the blood vessels in my eyes seemed to start leaking the next day.

When Mabel brought me dinner the weekend after the surgery and I could barely see her, she'd gone quiet and left as soon as she'd eaten the last bite from her plate. Later, when I went to work to get the last of my belongings so that I could start my abrupt retirement, people either didn't talk to me or they spoke to me like I was dying. After the incident with the cans at the grocery store, I'd had enough. I stopped leaving my house, and only Nathan and Marney were allowed to enter.

After Marney sent Mabel away, I said I'd send her back to her mom if she ever tried something like that again. Marney had apologized, and I'd forgiven her as soon as I heard the tears creep into her voice.

"Okay," I said and reached for the plate, "but only this once. Don't ask me again."

Marney jumped to her feet. "No cheating," she said. "I know you can see pretty well with these bright bulbs." I didn't tell her that even with them, the world had almost completely disappeared.

I stabbed something with my fork and brought it to my lips. It was bland, both slimy and gritty. I grabbed the napkin from my lap and spat it out. "The taste is why I don't eat those damn things."

"But you know what it is?"

"I don't think it's fair to test me like this. How many people eat avocados for dinner? In the middle of winter. They taste even worse off season."

"I wanted to give you something easy the first time."

"Okay, you made your point. I want to eat something real now."

Marney grabbed a plate off the counter. "There," she said, pushing it in front of me. "You figure it out."

Her footsteps retreated across the hall, behind her bedroom door, then stopped. The bedsprings squeaked, and again, before settling. I held my head cocked, hoped I didn't look like those blind musicians sitting behind their pianos, their necks bent at odd angles, broad grins across their faces. The way their heads swung back and forth as the music moved them. This was the first time Marney had talked back to me. I wasn't sure what I thought of it.

I shoved my fork into the middle of the plate where it hit porcelain. For a second I thought it was empty but then realized that Marney had set the food around the edges. I'd talked about this with Nathan, how some people liked it arranged on the sides, others with something in the middle. I didn't care, as long as I could eat.

I speared a piece of meat and put it into my mouth. It was stringy but moist, maybe roast? Or pork loin? Could even be squirrel, which I'd eaten as a girl. I was no good at this game. What if Marney had given me possum, guessing I wouldn't know the difference? I put my fork down and pushed back from the table.

"Not hungry?" Marney asked.

"I can't eat it if I don't know what it is," I said.

"What do you think it is?"

I didn't answer. Marney walked around the table, her footsteps reverberating through the floor and up into my chair. She sat and took a bite of something from her own plate. "I know what it is."

"Don't you think I know that? Your job isn't to trick me. It's to help me, so help, dammit."

"Help yourself," she said.

I sighed. "First I thought roast, then maybe a pork loin. It's kind of like squirrel, but I figure it could just as easily be possum."

"Possum? You think I would serve you possum?"

"Who knows?" I threw my hands up. "I don't know you. I babysat your mom thirty years ago, and now you live in my house. My head's full of thoughts about how I'm going to live when you're gone, and I can't even see your red hair anymore unless we stand in the sunlight." I felt a few stray tears on my face. I wasn't crying, not really, but my eyes had sprung leaks. They were betraying me every time I turned around.

"Pot roast," Marney said. "I put it in the crock pot with carrots and potatoes, which are mixed together at the bottom of your plate. But now it's cold."

She picked up my plate and put it in the microwave. We ate dinner in silence.

* * *

After weeks of working through the books with Marney, my eyesight, almost completely gone, had become an afterthought. I rarely turned on the 150-watt bulbs that Marney had installed throughout the house. I didn't know the last time I'd flicked the switch in my bedroom. My fingers were more nimble, my organization better. I remembered where things were, learned to gauge Marney's mood by the force of her footsteps instead of trying to make out the expression on her face. Learned to decipher food by taste and texture. Never expected anything to be as it should be but instead to anticipate that nothing would be as it should. Learned to control my own fall.

I stood at the counter chopping onions and tried to think of a way to show Marney that she was succeeding, that her books and the way she wheedled me with her tears helped. Without her, I wouldn't be cutting vegetables, would have still been afraid of knives. I owed her.

After breakfast, we'd venture into town. I would help with the grocery shopping that Marney usually did on her own, learning to move among other people and maneuver in unfamiliar places. Since Marney arrived, I hadn't left the house, had let her take care of everything. But Marney wouldn't be there forever. I tried to push my fear away as I sliced vegetables for our omelets.

I heard Marney's heavy footsteps move from the bathroom toward her bedroom, smelled the steamy scent of a woman freshly showered. I cracked the eggs against the rim of a mixing bowl and heard them splat in the bottom. I poured the milk slowly, as I listened to Marney moving around her room, getting ready for our day on the town.

In the car, I sat with my hands in my lap and said nothing.

"Are you okay?" Marney asked.

"Fine," I said. "I'll be fine."

"You're sure?" she asked.

"I said so, didn't I?"

We didn't speak the rest of the drive.

"It's going to be busy in here," Marney said as she pulled into a parking space. "Maybe we should try somewhere quieter."

"No, we can start here. If it's too much, we'll try something else next time."

Marney reached across the car and put her hand on top of mine. "There's no reason to push yourself. We have time."

"I'll be fine," I said. "You're the one who's been forcing me to grow up. Now it's your turn."

Marney let go of my hand. "Be careful getting out."

I swung the door open and planted my feet on the ground. Marney already stood beside me, breathing heavily. "Let me have your arm," she said, "just for the parking lot. After that you're on your own."

I didn't argue. We moved toward the store, my knees shaking, Marney whispering minor obstacles in my ear. I tried to maneuver naturally. When my feet met the sidewalk in front of the store, I shook my arm loose.

The amazing thing was how I could feel people around me, sense their presence while only seeing vague shapes. Inside, I wouldn't even have the shapes because of the fluorescent lighting. Still, I'd have that extra sense I was slowly acquiring, where my ears heard the low hum of pant legs rubbing together and my body felt the heat of others. It didn't work perfectly yet. Sometimes I didn't even know when Marney entered a room. But it was a beginning.

The doors opened with a whoosh, which seemed louder now, more present.

"The carts are about five feet straight ahead, slightly to your right," Marney whispered.

I moved forward, my right arm extended a little, and felt my hand hit the edge of a cart. I touched the surface, cold metal that had recently been outside, and moved along until I found the plastic handle. I pulled it out, taking a big step back.

Marney moved to my side and said, "Directly to your right."

I maneuvered the cart toward the door and felt my feet move from indoor/outdoor carpet to smooth linoleum. "Okay," I said. "What's first?"

"We need lettuce and mushrooms."

I thought back to the map I'd memorized. Marney had brought it home and quizzed me until I could tell her what each aisle contained. There was no way for me to memorize where each item was located on the shelf, but Marney had been right. I felt more in control knowing the general vicinity of everything.

I started to move to my right, then heard someone cry out at the same time my cart hit an obstacle. I stopped and said, "Are you hurt?" I faced the direction the bump had come from. My cheeks felt warm.

Silence, then a man cleared his throat. "Sorry about that." I listened to the rustle of his pants as he hurried away.

Marney came to my side and whispered, "You okay?"

"I think I could have run him over and kept going."

"You should have seen his face. I don't think he knew what to do."

"The pleasures of being blind," I said and smiled. My face was cooling, and I wondered at this new sort of power. "Which first, lettuce or mushrooms?"

* * *

At the register, I took out my wallet, a new one with separate sections for different bills. I pulled each one out and held them in the air in front of me until I felt a small tug on the other end. I shoved the change in my pocket for Marney to sort later.

I'd messed up a few times, running into other people or their carts, once even knocking the corner off a display. But I was out in public again. At the door, Marney and I both took hold of the cart's handle.

We stepped onto the sidewalk, and I leaned my weight on the cart, tired. "The ramp is to your left," Marney said.

We maneuvered down the small ramp. I chose my steps carefully, but the next thing I knew, I tripped and was going down. I pushed the cart away from me. Then, I loosened my body, let myself fall. My hands slid across gravel. My face met the ground, and pain exploded in my cheekbone as it grated against the asphalt.

I took my time and felt for pain in each limb before trying to sit up. My face and hands burned, but at least no bones seemed to be broken.

"Agnes, Agnes," Marney said. When I could feel she was close, I said, "I'm fine," but felt warm wetness on my cheek. Reaching my hand up, I felt the blood drip and cover my fingers. I'd given myself more of a cut than I'd suspected. Marney moaned and called out, "Can someone help us? Please?" Then, Marney squatted to the ground beside me and began to cry.

I reached toward her with my clean hand and patted her face, first hitting her nose and then caressing her cheek. "It's okay," I said. But I felt her tears on my fingers.

"I'm sorry," Marney managed. "I can't do this."

I heard people approaching us, their footsteps a deep vibration. "But you are doing it. We're doing it."

POPULAR

—

Clara showed up at my house with gym bags full of clothes, makeup, curling irons, hairspray, shoes, and anything else that might make us beautiful enough to go to the Brickton Fair. She looked through my closet and shook her head. "You can wear my clothes, Rachel," Clara said in a voice that was oddly throaty, almost sultry, for a fifteen-year-old. "I'll do your makeup too," she added.

She emptied mountains of clothes onto my bed and dressed me in one outfit after another until she was satisfied. Clara's skinny jeans fit me like a second skin—she had no curves, while my hips and boobs had appeared out of nowhere over the summer. "Sexy," she proclaimed. "They sure don't look like that on me." She checked out her nonexistent butt in the mirror. She found a red halter top on the bottom of her pile of clothes and finished off my new look with four-inch platforms.

"We're going to the parade, right?" I asked. She nodded. I said I couldn't walk so far in those shoes.

It was a mile from my house to the parade, and I usually skipped it. My parents said it wasn't worth the walk to hear fire engines and the high school band making so much noise. "I'll start a fire if you want to hear sirens," Dad always said. But Clara said the parade was our chance to scope everyone out. We would be going into our sophomore year of high school, and this was our chance to see how much everyone had changed over the summer and get first dibs on the guys who'd grown into their man-sized feet.

"You don't wear platforms when you walk," Clara said and rolled her eyes. "You wear flip flops and change when we get there."

"Oh," I said. I was still learning the rules. The year before, I hadn't been on Clara's radar, but now that I'd filled out and persuaded my mom to let me straighten my hair, she'd decided to befriend me. Once she learned that I lived on the hill above the fairgrounds and that I could have a week-long sleepover, I'd supplanted Jasmine as her best friend. I wasn't always sure that I liked Clara, but her life was more exciting than mine. I usually went to school and played basketball with the kids on my street in the afternoon. Clara talked to boys and tried on new shades of lipstick. I wanted to try on her life for a while.

I'd always wanted to be popular, and at Brickton High there were two ways to do that, become a cheerleader or be hot enough that all the guys wanted you. I'd tried out for the cheer squad at the end of my freshman year, but I didn't have the gymnastics skills. I could do a decent round-off, but those girls were doing back handsprings and full tucks. I quickly learned that to be a high school cheerleader, you needed to go to cheer camp and gymnastics classes from elementary school on. My parents didn't have the time or money for that, never had, so now I'd turned my attention to the only other way I knew to be popular.

My mom stared as we walked down the stairs, our hair sleek, eyes done in layers of mascara and eye shadow, lips lined and filled in, clothes that hugged my curves and showed off Clara's mile-long legs. Mom's eyes were wide and worried. She opened her mouth to say something, but I shook my head. She smiled instead, though I knew it was fake. "Well, you girls sure look grown."

"Thanks, Mrs. Peters. I hope you don't mind. I made Rachel up."
Clara beamed. She knew the right thing to say. The worry in my mom's
eyes faded.

"You look so sophisticated," Mom said to me. "I wasn't ready for
that."

"Mom," I said and blushed.

"We'll be home as soon as the fair closes," Clara said and grabbed
my hand.

"I'd rather—," Mom started, but Clara and I were already running
out the front door. I'd never been allowed to stay at the fair past ten, but
I was fifteen. I was old enough.

We stood by the dentist's office for the parade, but before it started
we replaced our flip flops with platform shoes for me and heels for Clara.
She waved at boys I'd only looked at before, never daring to speak. "Look
at Jimmy D. walking with his mom," she said and laughed. "Guess nothing changed over the summer." When Jimmy looked over at us, he saw
Clara laughing and continued on his way. I stood a little behind Clara
when friends of my parents walked by, hoping they wouldn't see me,
and if they did, that they wouldn't recognize me under all the makeup.
I didn't want her to make fun of me too.

"Look," she said and cocked her head toward Ben March who was
walking down the opposite side of the street with a guy I didn't know.
She waved at the boys, and they walked toward us.

Clara grabbed my arm. "I get Ben. You take the other one."

I nodded.

"He's cute," Clara said. "He might be new. Or Ben's cousin. It doesn't
really matter. This is your chance."

"My chance?"

"It's not enough to look the part," Clara said. "You need a boyfriend."

A boyfriend. I'd never had one before, never even been kissed. It
was kind of embarrassing, really. Even Melanie Jensen, who had acne

and didn't shave under her arms, had kissed Andy Killingsworth. He
had bad breath and body odor, but still. I was woefully behind everyone
in my grade when it came to that stuff. And the guy crossing the street
toward us was cute.

"This is Max," Ben said. "He's new."

"You remember Rachel?" Clara said. Ben looked at me, but I obviously hadn't registered freshman year. "She's kind of new too," Clara
added and laughed.

She didn't look the least bit nervous talking to Ben, though she'd
already filled me in that they were boyfriend/girlfriend in ninth grade
but hadn't seen each other over the summer, so she wasn't sure if they
still were. I glanced at Max and looked away again. He was staring at
me. I blushed.

"Max," Clara said and nudged me. "Where are you from?"

"Ohio," he said.

"Why'd you move to West Virginia?" I asked.

He smiled. Boys didn't usually smile at me. I grinned and lifted my
chin. Clara wrapped her arm around Ben's and started walking down
the sidewalk, ignoring the parade completely, not that we'd paid much
attention to anything but the fair queen contestants anyway. When
the cheerleading squad passed by, Clara laughed and aped their move-
ments, waving her arms in the air. Ben cheered her on. I decided not to
tell Clara that I'd tried out. Max and I watched Clara's show but didn't
join in. I didn't tell him that I thought the cheerleaders were graceful,
that I'd always wanted to be so popular.

At first, Max and I didn't touch at all, kept at least a foot between
us, but after he laughed at something I said, I inched closer, and my arm
brushed his. He talked all the way to the fairgrounds. I nodded and said,
"Really?" or "Hmmm," when I thought I should.

* * *

The sound of songs that had been popular the year before blared from giant speakers, and strobe lights from some of the bigger rides flickered across the faces of people who passed by. We could see them, but they couldn't see us. We sat outside the fence of the public pool, on the edge of the fairgrounds, hidden in the shadows. The concrete was damp, and there was nowhere to lean back, but Clara had claimed this spot for the week. We were its queens. People from school dropped in and out all evening, but Clara and Ben and Max and I were staples. Every time a boy looked at me, Max scooted closer. Once, he put his arm around me. I liked it.

Max pulled out a pack of cigarettes and offered one to me. I looked at Clara who nodded, so I accepted. I'd never smoked before. Max held the flame to my cigarette first, and I sucked on it when the fire met its tip. The smoke filled my mouth, but as it hit my throat and then my lungs, a cough exploded from me, and the cigarette flew through the air and landed on the ground. I leaned forward as tears of pain sprung to my eyes, and ropes of spittle hung from my lips as I tried to stop the hacking and find my breath again. When I finally looked up, everyone was staring at me, Max laughing softly. So much for being cool.

"Like this," he said and lit his own cigarette, sucking smoke deep into his lungs and exhaling through his nose.

Clara and Ben followed suit before standing up and walking away from the fair, into the roped off playground that was normally open but was closed for the week. I followed the orange lights of their cigarettes until they ducked into one of the pavilions.

"Where are they going?" I asked.

"To be alone," Max said. "Do you want to be alone with me?"

No one was nearby. "We're already alone."

"Out there," he said and nodded toward the pavilions.

"No," I said. "Not right now."

"Later?" Max asked and kissed my neck.

"Maybe," I said and leaned away from him.

I looked toward the pavilions and then back at Max who was watching me. "You're not a sophomore," I said.

"I am," he said.

I ran my hand across his cheek, felt the stubble that I'd noticed earlier. "Boys our age don't need to shave."

"I'm not a first time sophomore," he said. "School's not really my thing."

I didn't tell him that I loved school. I didn't know what else to say, so I looked at the lights of the rides behind us. We'd paid to get into the fair and then come straight here, not even bothering to buy a funnel cake or get in line for the Tilt-a-Whirl. Now, the music was beginning to slow, some of the rides closing up for the night. It had to be close to eleven. My mom would be waiting.

"Let me show you," Max said, and I thought maybe we'd go into the lights instead of sitting on the damp ground beside the pool, but he shoved his cigarette into my hand. "Don't breathe it in," he said. "Just fill your mouth up with smoke and blow it out."

It took four tries before I could do it without hacking. It tasted bad, but I liked it. The smoke made me feel lightheaded and bold, like I could do anything. "Give me another," I said. Max lit it and handed it to me. The butt was wet with his spit.

We were halfway through our second cigarettes when Clara came back, Ben's arm wrapped around her waist, the tips of his fingers inside the tops of her shorts. Her hair was messy, and I wondered how far she'd gone.

"We should go soon," she said to me. "You two say your goodbyes."

I nodded and started to stand up.

"Don't hurry," Ben said. "You've got a few minutes."

I looked over at Max, and he leaned in, his mouth already halfway open. I didn't quite know what to expect, but his tongue was in my mouth as soon as his lips met mine, and I tried to move my lips in response to his. His whiskers were rough against my face. After what felt like hours, he leaned back and smiled softly. "I'll see you tomorrow?" he asked.

I nodded. It didn't really matter whether he liked school. I liked him.

* * *

Clara and I sat across my bed from one another, comparing notes on the night before.

"You can't spend the whole week by the pool," she said.

I was glad. After two nights of nothing but cigarettes and sloppy kisses, I was getting bored. I wanted to get cotton candy and eat it on the Ferris wheel while Max held my hand. I wanted him to hit a balloon with darts until he won me a stuffed animal.

"You're being a cock tease," Clara said.

"A cock tease?"

"Max told Ben you gave him blue balls."

I was too embarrassed to ask what that meant.

"Don't just sit there," Clara said. "You've gotta do something about it."

"Like what?" I asked.

"Fuck him," she said.

"No way," I said. She couldn't mean it. I wasn't trying to wait until I was married or anything, but I'd only known Max a few days.

"Rachel," Clara said, "this is serious. Max already asked if I have other friends."

My stomach dropped. I couldn't picture tagging along with Clara and Ben. They didn't need a third wheel, and I liked Clara's life better than my old one. Boys looked at me. Older girls, seniors, nodded like they knew me. But apparently that wasn't enough to be popular. "What do I do?" I asked.

"Take him to the park," she said. "Back to the pavilion. At least give him a blowjob."

"Gross," I said. "What do I do?"

Clara burst out laughing.

"Where do you learn this stuff?" I asked.

"What stuff?"

"What to do with guys. How to dress. How to put on makeup." I threw up my hands. At school, I always knew the answers, but here I was failing. No wonder I'd never had a boyfriend. I didn't even know what to do with one.

"Sucking dick is just like sucking a finger," Clara said. "A little different, but the same idea. I'll show you. I'll show you all of it."

* * *

I let Max unbutton the front of my shirt and felt his hands fumble with my bra clasp before he gave up and pushed the cups above my breasts. "Wow," he said, and I smiled, but he never looked at my face. Instead, he grabbed my boobs in his hands and stuck his face in between them.

I wondered if he could hear my heart beating. I could. I was trying to remember what Clara had told me, trying to do it all right. Max's kissing and grabbing excited me, but sometimes my mind wandered as I thought about what she'd told me to do next.

"Oh baby," I whispered and moaned a little.

Max seemed to like it. He pushed me onto the concrete floor. My head thumped against the ground, but he didn't notice. He was rubbing up against me, and I arched my back, pressing closer to him. Part of me wanted to shove him off me, tell him we were moving too fast.

He pulled his T-shirt over his head, and I knew I shouldn't let him go much further. Then, the words "cock tease" echoed in my head, and I realized I couldn't stop. If he was upset about having blue balls before, he wouldn't forgive me now.

I remembered Clara telling me to take some initiative, so I unzipped his jeans. The head of his penis poked up through his underwear, and I grabbed it with both hands. Max groaned. "Gentle," he said. "Gentle."

That's when he started pulling my pants down, and I started to pull them back up but instead whispered, "There's a condom in the pocket of my jeans."

"Don't worry," Max said. "You can't get pregnant your first time."

I knew he was wrong, and I started to say something but stopped. Clara said to go along with him, to make him feel good, like he was in charge. I kicked my jeans off my feet and put my hands around his head, pulling him toward me.

Before I knew what he was doing, I felt his knee spread my thighs, and then he shoved himself inside me. Clara had warned me that it might hurt the first time, but I was surprised at how much it burned. I felt like he was ripping me from the inside. I wrapped my knees around him, let out moans when it hurt too much, and didn't let him see the tears in my eyes. He started to push harder and faster and made grunting noises. I tried to move my hips in pace with his but couldn't, so I stopped and let him jerk my body around as he wanted. Then, he yelled out, and I knew this was the moment Clara had described. It would be over soon if I just waited.

It was. He froze and fell in a heap on top of me before looking at my face and grinning.

"Oh, baby," he said and kissed me. He rolled off me and stood, still half-dressed, his pants and underwear shoved down below his ass, his shoes still on. "I'll be right back," he said and ducked outside the pavilion.

After a minute, I heard piss hit the ground and grabbed my purse where I found a maxi pad and stuck it to my panties. Clara had been right to give it to me—I could already feel something on my inner thighs. By the time I heard Max's zipper, I was back in my pants and had my bra over my breasts. All I had to do was button my shirt, but my hands shook.

Max grabbed me and hugged me against his still bare chest. "Rachel," he said. "I love you."

"I love you too," I said.

Max put his shirt on, took a cigarette for himself, and handed one to me. I held it between my teeth while he lit it, then buttoned my shirt. We walked out of the pavilion, trailing cigarette smoke behind us. If Clara had been looking, she would have spotted us by the glowing orange lights.

JAWS OF LIFE

—

"Where are we?" Iris asked.

"You have a doctor's appointment," Harold said again. "Remember?"

"Oh," she said and stared into space.

As the hospital elevator rose, Harold leaned back and closed his eyes. He was tired, but when they slowed to a stop, he stood upright. The reception desk faced the elevator, and Harold wondered if its placement was for patients who were sent up alone, their family members pushing a button and then taking a much-needed break.

"Mrs. Travers?" the nurse said.

Iris didn't react. "That's us, sweetie," Harold said and guided her out of the elevator. Not that he expected a reaction. Iris's moments of lucidity had seeped away, leaving a confused old woman who didn't recognize herself or anyone around her.

"Can you keep an eye on her?" he asked the nurse.

She peered at him. "Are you feeling okay, Mr. Travers?"

"Fine," he said. "I'm fine. I forgot something in my truck. I'll be right back."

When she nodded, he squeezed Iris's hand, but she didn't respond. He sighed. Iris looked like his wife, the woman who'd once picked him up from work and driven past their exit on the interstate, who'd continued driving all the way to the beach where they bought bathing suits and toothbrushes and spent a long weekend swimming and eating crab cakes. She looked like that woman, but she wasn't anymore.

In the elevator, he told himself to stop, to go back. On his way to the truck, he convinced himself that he needed the paperback he'd left under the seat. Even sitting behind the wheel, he told himself to get out and return to his wife. Instead, Harold turned the key in the ignition, put the truck into drive, and inched toward the hospital's exit. On the road, he managed to tell himself that he was only taking a short drive. That Iris's appointment would last thirty minutes. As long as he was back by then, no one would ever know.

Harold felt older than his seventy years. His joints ached, and his eyes burned. It took him a few extra minutes to get up from a chair, and he hadn't been able to kneel in almost a decade. All he wanted was to fish on Saturdays and spend Sundays playing pinochle at the Elks. He wanted to watch TV in between naps and open his first beer at three. Instead, he put combination locks on the inside of their doors and reminded Iris who he was, who she was. And for a long time he didn't mind. He'd been more than willing to take care of Iris, to make sure her final years were painless. He'd even told her, right after her diagnosis, "I'm here until the very end." And he had meant it. He had taken care of everything the first decade she was sick, when she still had moments of lucidity, before she started calling, "Harold! Harold!" every time he left her alone in a room. When he'd run back to reassure her, Iris didn't recognize him. She didn't know the man whose hair had long turned gray, whose eyes were lost in a sea of wrinkles, whose stomach lapped over his belt. She expected the man Harold had been, the one she'd married thirty years before, when they'd both been young. Not the old man he'd become. Of course, it had been months since Iris yelled for him, when she still remembered that she had a husband. Now, he'd give anything for her to call out to him, even if it was only a memory of him.

He and Iris had met at a support group for people who'd lost their spouses. Her first husband had had a stroke and died at the dinner table a few years before. "Forty's too young to die," she'd said, and Harold put his hand over hers. She smiled.

After the meeting, they went out for coffee. As soon as they sat down, Harold said, "I'm not a widower." He explained that he'd never been married, hadn't been on a date in years, that a friend had told him he needed to meet a widow. "And this is the only way I knew to find one. You can't walk up to women on the street asking if they're widows. And you're nice. My friend was right."

He'd ignored the cup of coffee, but after his speech, Iris added sugar and milk into both their cups and stirred. She pushed one toward him and said, "Well, that's one I haven't heard before." And then she laughed. A deep belly laugh that made people turn and stare. A laugh so contagious that Harold chuckled too. Until the whole situation became so absurd that they giggled until Harold's face hurt and Iris was gasping for breath.

They were married six months later.

Once, Harold had taken her to the Brickton Fair. He bought lemonade and a handful of tickets. He gave the tickets and a fifty-dollar bill to a ride operator. They rode the Ferris wheel for hours, only getting off when the fair began to shut down for the night. On the ground, they felt like they were still moving in slow circles. Iris said it was the best date ever, even if they were already married. After that, they went to any fair that came to the area, even if only to ride the Ferris wheel and leave. Harold still loved Ferris wheels, though he hadn't been on one in years. They belonged to his life with Iris.

He pointed his truck toward the interstate, but he approached the onramp and drove past it. He merged with the traffic moving toward downtown Morgantown, the stop-and-go movement soothing to him at the moment, when he had to decide his next move. If he got on the interstate, he would keep going, past the exit for his house, through the mountains, until the hills petered out and he found himself on the shore. He wouldn't be able to stop. Behind the seat sat a bag with a change of clothes and a toothbrush. He kept it there for emergencies, like the night Iris had cut herself with a kitchen knife and had to get stitches. She'd been so agitated at the hospital that they'd sedated her and kept her overnight. Harold had slept by her bed and refilled his overnight bag the next day when they'd returned home. He'd needed it again when Iris got out of bed in the middle of a January night and walked down the street barefoot. He'd found her the next day, asleep under a child's swing in the park, her toes and cheeks frostbitten. They'd spent longer in the hospital then, and Iris had lost her pinkie toe. That was when he put the combination locks on the front and back doors.

Ahead, downtown Morgantown loomed, a small cluster of buildings surrounded by the university and suburbs. Harold crested the hill and slammed on the brakes. A line of cars was stopped just past the summit. The little Mazda behind him managed to stop without hitting him, its brakes squealing, but the truck behind it saw the stalled traffic too late. Frame jacked up, tires topping four feet, the truck climbed the rear of the little car and crushed the roof before coming to a complete stop. Harold watched in horror as the driver seemed to be crushed, the windshield buckling and bursting outward, the support beams bending, until it was difficult to believe the car had ever been more than a flattened mess.

Harold jumped out of his truck. He ran to the car and saw an arm pinned in the metal. The nails were bright red, a class ring on the fourth finger. "Are you okay in there?" he called.

"Hello?" he heard. It was faint.

"I hear you," he said.

"I didn't see her," someone behind him said. "I tried to stop. I did." The voice trailed away.

"Are you okay?" he asked.

"I'm stuck," the woman said. "Get me out." Her voice was frantic, rising in pitch.

Harold gripped her hand, and she squeezed back. He couldn't see the rest of her, but the hand was strong. "Help is on the way," he said. "Is there anyone in the car with you?"

"No," she said. "I'm alone." He heard a muffled sob.

He rubbed his thumb in circles across her palm, the way he did to Iris's back, the one thing that could still calm her down.

Fluids dripped from the truck above, soaking his shirt. People stood near him, arguing over whether to move the truck. The driver's voice carried through the others and then faded. The sirens were still distant.

"I'm Harold," he said into the wreckage. "What's your name?"

"Help me," she called.

"I am," he said. "Focus on my voice. Tell me who you are."

"Angie."

"Angie," he said. The sun beat down on his head, made him squint. "What were your plans today?"

"Plans?" she asked.

"Yes," he said. "Where were you going before the accident?"

"I don't want to die," she said, her breath too fast.

"You won't," he said. "I promise."

A moment of silence, then, "Class," she said. "I have an exam."

"At the university?"

"Yes," she said. "Who are you?"

"Harold," he said again. "I told you." He looked around at the people who stood nearby, but none stepped forward to help.

"What are you doing here?" she asked.

"I just dropped my wife off at the doctor."

"Is she okay?"

"No," he said. "She's not."

"I'm sorry," she said, and he realized the absurdity of telling his problems to a girl who might be dying. He had no clue what was happening in her car.

"Are you bleeding?" he asked. "Can you feel your toes?"

"What's wrong with her?" Angie asked.

"Can you move at all?"

"What's wrong with your wife?"

"She has Alzheimer's." Sweat ran down the back of his head, to his neck, into the collar of his shirt.

"Oh," she said. "I'm sorry," and squeezed his hand.

The sirens surrounded them now, so he didn't try to speak. Neither did she. The crowd around them had grown, and there were flares in the road. Ahead, his truck still stood with the driver's side door open.

A fireman rushed toward him. "Sir," he said, "I'm going to need you to step back."

Harold unclasped his fingers, but Angie gripped him tighter. "Don't leave me," she called.

"Ma'am," the firefighter said.

"Her name's Angie."

"Angie," he said. "You need to let go of this man's hand."

"No," she said.

The fireman stepped back and conferred with another man, both looking at Harold. He watched as police officers and firemen surrounded the vehicles and others told the onlookers to back away, until Harold was one of the few without a uniform.

"Harold?" Angie called.

"I'm right here," he said and squeezed her hand.

"I didn't study for my exam," she said.

"That's okay."

"I was going to copy off the girl in front of me. She writes big."

"I left my wife at the doctor's office," he said.

Angie didn't respond.

"I'm a horrible person," he said.

"No, you're not," she said. "You've stayed here with me."

"I wasn't planning on picking my wife up from the doctor. I was going to leave her there."

"That's kind of bad," she said.

"Yes," he agreed. "It is."

"You won't leave me, will you?" Angie asked.

"I'll stay 'til the end," he said.

The firemen were moving now, ready to remove the truck from Angie's car. Police officers spoke into radios attached to their belts. Paramedics jumped from an ambulance that had just arrived and ran toward Harold. "You need to step back, sir," one said. "We have this."

"No," Angie called.

"I'm not going anywhere," Harold said to her. "I'm staying with you."

"Sir," the man said again. "I can't help her with you here. You need to move."

"I don't want to die alone," she yelled. "Don't let me die alone."

"You won't die," he said. "I promise."

She squeezed his hand one last time, and he let go. He stepped back, pulled down the tailgate on his truck, and sat. The firemen pulled machines from their truck, and a paramedic grasped the hand Harold had just released. Another group of men hooked chains to the truck.

He watched the rescue attempt, as first the truck was lifted from the crushed car, then attached to a tow truck. The firemen moved forward with the Jaws of Life. The roof of the car was so crushed it looked like Angie had been driving a convertible. A paramedic ducked beside the door and kept an eye on her vitals.

Harold blinked back tears, watched the flutter of Angie's fingers, tried to believe that she would be okay. The men used giant hydraulic scissors to snip the top of the car away, until Angie's head poked up. She was younger than Harold had thought, no more than nineteen. She wore streaks of blonde and pink in her dyed-black hair, and trails of mascara clung to her cheeks. Even from this far away, he could see that her tears had washed away a thick layer of makeup.

"Angie," he called and waved. She looked at him, and her eyes filled with tears.

A paramedic slipped an oxygen mask over her face and tended to her arm, which already had a giant black and purple bruise across the area where the car's roof had pinned it. The firemen moved on to cutting the dashboard from around her lap. The sun beat down on Harold's bald head. He needed water and a hat, but he didn't move. It had been at least an hour since he'd left the doctor's office.

As the final pieces of the car were removed from Angie's legs, he watched the paramedics move in, sliding her onto a backboard, tending to legs that looked misshapen from the car's weight. She kept her eyes on his as they rushed her to the ambulance.

"Wait," Angie yelled and pulled the oxygen mask from her face. The paramedics tried to replace it, but she shook them off. With her good arm, she pointed toward Harold. "He's coming with me."

Harold stood and took a step toward her. He would ride with her, hold her hand the whole way.

"Are you family?" the paramedic asked him.

Harold opened his mouth to speak, but Angie said, "He's my granddad."

He grabbed her hand and nodded while he held back tears. He was old enough to be her grandfather. He just hadn't thought of himself that way.

Angie let the paramedic replace the oxygen mask, and Harold

climbed into the ambulance. He sat on one side of Angie, while the paramedic sat on the other. Angie closed her eyes but didn't let go of Harold's hand. He used his other hand to smooth the hair back from her forehead. He realized they were heading back the hospital where he'd left Iris. His pulse quickened.

"It's crazy," the paramedic said once they were moving. "Her car looks like it went through a compactor, but she'll probably get out of the hospital today, tomorrow at the latest."

Angie looked almost fine. The backboard was a precaution, and her arm was probably broken, but somehow the car had created a cocoon around her, rather than crushing her. She'd be bruised and sore, but alive. Whole.

When they reached the emergency room, the ambulance's back doors opened. The paramedics pulled Angie's gurney out, and Harold followed. He walked beside her as they pushed her into the ER, but when they approached the double doors into the treatment area, a nurse stepped forward. She put her hand against Harold's chest. "You'll need to wait over there," she said and pointed to a row of chairs.

"I can't leave her," Harold said. "I promised."

"Yes, you can," Angie said and let go of him. He reached for her hand, but it was already too far away.

The doors swung shut, and Angie disappeared from his sight. Harold started toward the chairs and then stopped. He walked to the elevator. Once the car arrived, he stepped inside, his ascent swift.

MUDDIN'

———

Though they weren't married anymore, Chelle and Bill still got together for sex from time to time. But only when they had both been drinking at the Elks, usually on nights when the special was tequila. Cheap tequila with a little lime and salt was Chelle's favorite. After the first few shots, when Chelle said, "That's it for me. I don't want to crawl home," Bill would send a shot over to her table, then another. He would bring the third one himself.

They still liked each other when they were sober, but they only remembered how much they'd been in love when they were drunk. Then, it was as if they were still in high school and a bottle of Matador and a starry sky were all they needed to believe they were meant to be together. The wedding they'd had after a positive pregnancy test, the stillbirth months later, the intervening years of loving and hating each other until the hate outweighed the love—all that disappeared when Bill bought her drinks and put his hand on her leg under the table. Then, they remembered the nights Chelle had stopped believing she killed their baby and the years they'd spent trying to make a new one. Eventually, Chelle had come to believe she was defective. That was when the love had turned into hate. It had been a relief to end the marriage when they were thirty; there was no point in trying to make something work that obviously didn't. But every once in a while, when the sky was clear and the tequila went down smoothly, they were eighteen again, and what mattered most was getting each other's clothes off as quickly as possible.

"Let's go muddin'," Chelle said one night after sex. They were at her house, formerly their house, in her bed, which had also been their marriage bed. Bill lay on his back, still breathing heavily, but that was more from years of smoking and working in the coal mines than from the sex, which had been quick and unimaginative. He sat up, lit two cigarettes, and passed one to her.

"I'm too drunk," Bill said.

"You're just the right amount of drunk." Chelle swung her leg around and sat on Bill's chest, straddling him. "It'll be like it used to be."

At the moment, she was almost drunk enough to believe it and that their fifteen minutes of sex had been like it was years before. Then they'd made love for hours, or at least touched and licked each other for hours, kept each other excited for whole nights.

"Your car?" Bill asked.

"Still at the Elks."

"Okay," he said. "But I'm driving."

"We always were good together," she said.

"We still are."

Chelle didn't bother with a bra—she threw a sweatshirt over jeans and called it enough. It was still early spring, and though the days were warm enough for a T-shirt, the nights still dipped into the forties. Tonight, the moon was new and the sky was clear, millions of stars twinkling above them. With no cloud cover, it was also cold enough to see your breath, and the weatherman had called for frost.

As soon as Bill turned the key in the ignition, Chelle switched the heat to full blast.

Bill turned on the headlights and aimed them toward the trees. Chelle's doublewide sat on an acre of land surrounded by forest. She didn't own anything outside of that one cleared acre, but the Millers up the road let her use the woods when she wanted, except during deer season. Then, she wore orange even in her yard.

"Hold on tight," Bill yelled as they sped into the trees.

The truck jumped forward, plunging into mud holes and climbing out the other side, mud flying into the air, onto the windshield and back onto the truck. Bill turned on the wipers, but they just spread the mess, making it even harder to see. But that was part of the fun, moving between trees, sinking into the mud and then spinning the tires until you popped out, flying across the forest floor until you got hung up again and had to work your way out, never knowing exactly what was in front of you.

Ahead, Chelle saw what looked like a small pond. "Don't," she said.

"Don't what?"

"It's too deep. We'll get stuck."

Bill laughed, a booming belly laugh that filled the cab of the truck. Then, he gunned it, and Chelle's stomach lifted and dropped as the truck plunged into the mud, curtains of water spraying up, enveloping the windows. They climbed out of the hole, tires spinning, motor whining, and continued farther into the woods.

They were approaching areas Chelle had never seen before, beyond the Millers' land, onto someone else's, miles from Chelle's house. They sped up, the forest flashing by more quickly, saplings smacking the bumper and then disappearing. The truck bucked over mounds of earth, tree roots, and anything else that got in its way. Bill let out a yell as the truck slid across muddy grass and sideswiped a tree, knocking the side mirror off. Soon, Chelle was yelling along with him, both whooping at the darkness, feeling like the only ones alive in the empty night.

"I love you, baby," Bill yelled, and she said, "I love you, too." In that moment, they meant it.

There was another small pond ahead, but Chelle didn't yell out, and the truck dove into it easily enough, curtains of muddy water covering them again. But this time, when Bill gunned the engine to climb out the other side, the tires didn't catch hold. They spun in the mud, spewing water and chunks of earth behind them, while the truck sank into the muck. Bill downshifted and tried again, but the truck only settled more deeply into the earth.

"Wait," Chelle yelled over the whine of the motor, and Bill stopped and swore. Now almost completely underwater, the headlights dimmed. Chelle looked down and saw that the water had risen into the cab, covering her feet. She climbed onto the seat, but it was too late—her canvas sneakers were completely drenched. "Goddammit, Bill," she said, but he ignored her.

"I can't open the door," he said. He stuck his head out the window.

"No shit. I'll go out the back." Chelle opened the window in the back of the cab, and Bill pushed her through. It was cold enough that she could see her breath. The stars were bright above her. She shivered and wrapped her arms around her chest, cursing herself for not bringing a jacket.

Already, muddy water had started to seep through the tailgate and into the bed. She peered over the side and saw that the tires were almost completely buried in mud.

She rushed back to the window. "Turn it off, Bill."

"It's cold," he said. He held his hands over the heating vents. "Get back in so I can close the window."

She stuck one leg and then another through the window and said, "You've gotta turn the truck off."

"It's too damn cold for that."

"The water's too high. The exhaust is covered. You're gonna kill us."

He turned and looked out the back, peering past the bed. "You sure?"

In answer, she turned the key, and the truck was silent.

"I was gonna do it," Bill said.

"Not fast enough."

"It wouldn't kill us that quick."

Chelle's buzz had been wearing off for a while, and now she had a headache. "How do you know?" she asked.

"I just do. Besides, do you smell anything?"

"Carbon monoxide doesn't smell."

"Exhaust does."

Chelle leaned back and closed her eyes. "Did you bring your phone? We're gonna need a tow."

"No," Bill said. "We'll have to walk out."

"What about pushing it?"

"And how am I supposed to do that?"

"The usual way—you push, and I'll steer. Maybe the wheels can catch onto something."

"You saw how deep we are, didn't you?" he asked.

"We can still try," she said. It was cold and late, and she wanted to be back in her bed. Alone. She was too old for this.

"You push then. I'm not getting covered in mud."

"No way," she said.

"Exactly." He leaned back and crossed his arms over his chest. "We'll have to walk."

"Now?" Chelle asked.

"In the morning," Bill said.

"What am I supposed to do 'til then?"

"Keep warm."

Chelle was shivering in her thin sweatshirt and wet shoes. "That's easy for you to say. You've got extra insulation." She looked at Bill and the weight he'd put on since their divorce—his gut was bigger, and he had a layer of fat around his face and neck.

"Well, look at you sitting there like you're something special," he said. He smirked at her, one eyebrow raised, arms crossed. "Not all of us think eating's bad. You lose any more weight and you're gonna look like an orange skeleton, all that tanning. Ever think of eating a burger?"

"I eat," she yelled. "I can't help it." She'd always been skinny, no matter what she ate. And not sexy skinny either. She hadn't gotten boobs or her period until she was sixteen, and her hips had never filled out. She was built like a kid and still had to buy pants in the girls' section at the store. It was embarrassing walking around with glitter and stars on the butt of your jeans, but those were the only ones that fit.

Bill looked her up and down. "There's no cushion for the pushin'. If you didn't have hair down there, I couldn't touch you."

"Fuck you too," she said. "Mr. God-of-all-men. With that belly and the hair on your shoulders, I'm sure you have women everywhere trying to get on you."

"At least I don't go around pretending I'm perfect," he said. "You act like your shit don't stink, and now you're looking at me like it's all my fault we're out here. Remember, you're the one who wanted to go muddin'."

"I've never pretended I don't make mistakes," Chelle said. "I didn't say it was all your fault. I'll take my share of the blame."

"Like when you told me you only married me because you were knocked up?"

She lost her breath. "I didn't mean that," she said finally. "Not really."

He didn't answer or look in her direction.

"We both said a lot of things we didn't mean," she said.

"I'm going to try to get some sleep," he said. He leaned back in the seat, wrapped his arms around himself, and closed his eyes.

Chelle curled into a ball, but she couldn't get warm. She kicked her shoes off and stuck her bare feet in a crack in the seat. Then she pulled her arms inside her sweatshirt and wrapped them around her body to conserve heat. She pulled her shirt over her mouth, breathing warm air onto her chest, but the moisture made her shiver. Her whole body shook, and she couldn't stop.

"We were good together for a little while, weren't we?" Bill asked.

"For a few years, I'd say." She looked at him, but his eyes were still closed.

"You ever think what would've happened if we hadn't lost the baby?"

"I try not to," she said. Bill looked at her then, but Chelle turned away. "I did that enough when we were married."

"Do you—"

"Let's just try to get some sleep, okay?" she asked.

"Okay," Bill said. He looked at her, and she met his gaze. "Okay."

"I'm just tired," she said and leaned her head against the side window.

Though the truck had a bench seat, she tried to keep herself as far from Bill as possible. Sometimes, it hurt being this close to him. When they were drunk, they were fine, good together even, but when they were sober, as she was now, a lot of hurt came through. A lot of love as well, but she couldn't always separate the two. Tonight they felt like the same thing.

Chelle looked out the window, but between the trees and lack of moonlight, she couldn't even guess the way back to civilization. The stars glowed enough to see a few feet in front of her but not enough to judge which direction to take. Out here, houses sat on fifty or a hundred acres and you could walk for hours without running into another person if you didn't know where you were going.

"You won't make it back on your own," Bill said, as though reading her mind.

"I might."

"No," he said. "You won't. As soon as it's light, we'll be on our way."

"Watch me," Chelle said and tried to push the door open, but the water and mud had sealed it shut.

"Baby," Bill said. "Baby, please."

He reached for her, but Chelle shrunk against the door. "I'm not your baby," she said. "Let's just go to sleep." She pulled her knees to her chest again but couldn't stop shivering.

"You want to curl up together? We'll both stay warmer," Bill said.

She looked over, and Bill was watching her. She shook her head and turned away.

"It's gonna be a long night," he said.

It was cold enough that even the forest's normal nighttime noises were missing. Everything had dug a hole, built a nest, bundled up, and hunkered down for the night. Chelle and Bill were alone. She propped her back against the door, facing him.

"Have you dated anyone since we split up?" she asked.

"Dated?"

"Or slept with," she said.

"I slept with a couple women," he said.

"Oh."

"Did you think I wouldn't?"

"I never thought about it 'til now," she said.

"They weren't dates. They were both just one night." He was quiet. Then, "How about you?"

"I dated one guy for a while," she said.

"And?" Bill asked.

"He liked to travel, and he talked about the trips we'd take. I realized he could give me the kind of life I always dreamed of, the one we could never afford."

"I couldn't help getting laid off those times," Bill said.

"I'm not blaming you," Chelle said. "The thing is, this man offered me everything I thought I wanted."

"He sounds perfect," Bill said. There was an edge to his voice.

Chelle nodded. "Almost," she said. "But his hands were too soft. Like he'd never done a day of real work in his life. I wanted to hand him a shovel or something."

"I ruined you," Bill said.

"Yeah," Chelle said. "I guess you did."

She leaned her head back and closed her eyes. Bill pulled her feet out of the crack in the seat and rubbed them between his calloused hands. Chelle let him. She sat on her side of the truck's cab, he on his, but her feet had crossed into his territory, and Bill kept them warm. Like that, with one touch over years of distance, they fell asleep.

MAY OURS BE AS HAPPY
AS YOURS

———

Dad insisted we eat at Swan Song, a place my parents never went when married but where we met yearly to celebrate their divorce. The room was dark except for lights that shone on individual tables. Mom and Dad were framed in the glow of the bulb above them, smiling and staring at each other. Frank Sinatra crooned through wall-mounted speakers.

Mom looked surprised to see Stanley. I was too. I'd invited him, but I wasn't sure he'd really show. Mom blew kisses at us. She had pink circles of blush on her cheeks, and her red lipstick bled into the lines around her mouth. "I've missed you," Mom said to Stanley. "You never make it to our Sunday dinners."

"Sorry," Stanley said. "I've been working a lot of overtime."

We'd rehearsed our excuses beforehand. Stanley and I hadn't seen each other in weeks, though we'd talked over the phone a couple times. He'd spruced himself up since I'd moved out. His curls still stuck out in every direction, but with pressed dress pants and a nice button-down, they looked cute rather than messy. One of the reasons I'd left is because he hadn't changed a thing about himself since we got married. It was like he didn't feel the need to impress me anymore. At least until now.

"Looking good, you two," Dad said. "How's it going?"

"Great," I said. "We're really great. How about you?"

"It's a good day," Dad said, which he said every year. I never asked him if it was a good day because they were divorced or because they were together for dinner.

Dad was wearing the tie that he'd bought for his brother's funeral twenty years before, a strip of brown with bright pink ducks flying downward in a V. It was hideous. I hadn't seen it since Uncle Russell's funeral, and I never imagined he'd still have it. With their matching cowlicks and goatees, people used to think my father and his brother were twins, although Uncle Russell was ten years older. Dad always said that he had a career, while Russell only had jobs. Dad claimed that told us everything we needed to know about the two of them.

Instead of going on vacation, Mom, Dad, and I used to spend two weeks at Uncle Russell's house in Myrtle Beach every summer. Dad never mentioned careers and jobs while we were there, only when we returned home. We would swim in Uncle Russell's pool, make hamburgers on his grill, and play darts in his game room. Dad insisted we couldn't afford such a nice place if we'd paid for a vacation. For Mom, the centerpiece of our trip was Uncle Russell's speedboat. I didn't like how fast my uncle drove it, so Dad stayed home with me while Mom and Russell went out. Dad drank too much beer and watched me make sandcastles. Mom and Russell drove the boat up and down the coast for hours every morning. When they got back, her eyes were clear, her smile wide. Dad was usually drunk by then.

"What's up with the tie, Dad?" I asked.

"Nostalgia," Dad said.

He smiled at Mom, and she looked away, into the darkness beyond the tables.

Stanley cleared his throat. "Should we order something to drink?" he asked.

I glared at him. Poor Stanley. He hadn't even known that I was having an affair until I told him. "His name's Charles," I'd said. "How could you?" he asked, and before I could stop myself, I said, "Easily." The sad thing was, cheating on him really had been easy. He didn't even realize something had changed, and I wanted someone who wanted to be married to me, who acted like our marriage was an important part of his life. If he'd woken up one morning and I'd been replaced by a different woman, I'm not sure Stanley would have noticed.

"Let's at least order drinks," Stanley said and waved the waiter over.

"What's gotten into you?" I asked, but he was already asking the waiter about the wine selection. I wanted to ask him where this version of my husband had been all these years.

Mom still wasn't looking at us, and Dad shifted in his seat. My parents had divorced twenty years before, and the sudden appearance of Dad's ugly tie, which he hadn't worn in all these years, brought the end of their marriage abruptly to the table. I was ten when Uncle Russell died of a heart attack. When we walked into the funeral home for the viewing, Mom leaned over the body, hugged Russell around his chest, and bawled, tears streaming down her face. I stood behind her with Dad. He grabbed my hand and squeezed, cutting off the circulation to my fingers. I endured the pain as long as I could, but I had to pull my hand from his. He looked at me then, took my hand more gently, and we walked out of the funeral home and sat in the car until Mom came out. No one spoke on the drive home, eight hours without the radio and no talk of attending the burial the following day. Two weeks later, Dad packed up and moved out.

We hardly had any contact with Dad after the divorce, except the yearly dinners, where Mom dressed me in outfits covered with flowers and lace and pranced me around in front of him. They'd spend the whole meal fussing over me and ignoring one another, never quite looking each other in the eye. Even as a kid, I didn't trust their reasons for being so polite, but every year Mom told me that the dinners were for me, so that I would always remember how much my parents loved me. My parents weren't so awkward once I started bringing Stanley. Even when I explained that we were celebrating their divorce, Stanley acted like the dinners were a real celebration, like a wedding anniversary or a birthday party, letting all of us pretend as well.

Dad put his arm around Mom, whispered in her ear. She blushed. To look at them, no one would have guessed they were divorced, that for twenty years they had spoken only at these yearly parties.

Maybe I should have stopped myself, but something made me press forward. "That tie, Dad," I said, and Mom shot me a look that I ignored. "Can we talk about it?"

"Why would you want to talk about *that*?" Mom asked, her cheeks redder than before.

"Talk about what?" Stanley asked, but I didn't look at him. I'd never told him the whole story.

"It doesn't matter now, does it?" I asked Mom. "He forgave you."

No one said anything, so I leaned toward Dad. "You did forgive her, right?" Stanley looked at me and grabbed my arm, but I shook him off. "Right?" I asked again.

"This is supposed to be a celebration, Arlene," Mom said.

"Of what?" I asked.

"Freedom," Dad said.

"Family," Mom said. She glanced at Dad.

"What's going on?" I asked.

"What do you mean?" Mom asked.

"This," I said. Dad's arm was around Mom's shoulder, and she snuggled into him.

"We're dating," Dad said. Mom smiled, her eyes squinted into crescents. She kissed him on the cheek.

"You're divorced," I said.

"That doesn't mean we can't date," Mom said.

I wanted to tell them that Stanley and I were divorcing too. I wanted to let them know that I'd followed in Mom's footsteps, though not with Stanley's brother. I had more class than that.

"Congratulations," Stanley said. He shook my dad's hand, squeezed my mom's and smiled. He seemed genuinely happy for them. He waved the waiter over again and said, "A bottle of champagne."

"Instead of the wine?" the man asked.

"Yes. We're celebrating." He looked back at my parents. "I always thought you two were perfect for each other."

Mom reached over and ran her hands up and down the tie. Dad kissed her. I looked away, realized that they'd slept with Russell between them their whole marriage.

"So, you've forgiven her for everything?" I asked Dad.

"Really, Arlene?" Stanley asked. "Can't you just be happy for them?"

"Are you getting married again?" I asked.

"Does it matter?" Dad asked.

"It does to me," I said. Ever since they split up, I'd wanted my parents back together, but now I wanted to throw something at them, yell at them. Tell them that they weren't allowed to be happy when I wasn't.

"I don't know, Arlene," Mom said. She placed her palms flat on the table. "We weren't very happy when we were married."

"No," I said. "You weren't."

Stanley's smile faltered as he looked at each of us. Mom and Dad had scooted apart, and I looked down at the table. "I love being married," Stanley said.

"You do?" I asked.

"Of course," he said.

"What do you love about marriage?" Mom asked.

"That I'll never be alone," he said.

"You can still be alone," Dad said.

"I know that now," Stanley said. I looked at him, but he held my dad's gaze.

"It's the idea of marriage, right?" Dad said. "The idea that you'll always have someone?"

"But what happens if they leave?" Stanley asked. He didn't look at me, seemed to really want my dad's answer.

"At least you had them for a while," Dad said.

Stanley nodded.

"A friend of mine got married when she was eighteen," I said. "Remember, Mom? I was her maid of honor. They got engaged on Monday, and they were married on Wednesday. We bought her dress on Tuesday. When her mom asked her why she was hurrying, she said she was that excited to spend the rest of her life with him."

"See?" Stanley said. "That's what I mean."

"Are they still married?" Mom asked.

"No," I said. "They got divorced two years later. She had his initials tattooed on the back of her neck. She said she needed to find someone else with the same initials. I don't know if she ever did."

"That's sad," Mom said.

"What about love?" Dad asked. "Did your friend really love her husband, or was she young and in lust?"

"Love's the most important part," Mom said. "A marriage is doomed without it."

"But doesn't that go away after a while?" I asked. "Don't you get so comfortable you forget you were ever in love?"

"It can," Mom said. "You have to work to make sure it doesn't."

"I never stopped loving your mother," Dad said.

I couldn't speak. Tears welled in my eyes, and I watched Mom lean toward Dad. Their foreheads met, then their noses, then they kissed. Stanley slipped his handkerchief into my hand, and I wiped the tears off my cheeks.

I missed the ease of my marriage, the fact that Stanley knew I needed a handkerchief. Charles wouldn't have. I tried to picture him beside me at these dinners, and I couldn't. He would argue that marriage was a social institution, that you only got love if you were lucky, that he wasn't the marrying kind. He wouldn't understand that these dinners were a necessary tradition. That my family didn't make sense without them. Stanley understood all too well.

The waiter arrived with the champagne, and we watched as he popped the cork and then filled each of our glasses.

"To divorce," I said, raising my glass. My family turned toward me. "May everyone have one as fruitful as yours."

Stanley looked at my parents. "To divorce," he said. "May ours be as happy as yours."

We clinked glasses. I tilted my head back and swallowed every drop.

PHOTOGRAPHING THE DEAD

———

Silas Morgan saw the living in the dead and created something none of us could. When he was a child, if someone had told us how much we'd come to rely on him in years to come, we wouldn't have believed them. Through third grade, Silas never had friends, but he didn't seem to mind. His own company was enough. In fourth grade, though, he fell in love with his teacher Anita Pelland. She was already in her sixties by then and smelled of talcum powder. A lot of us had worked our way through elementary school with her at the head of the classroom. A few of us had adored her, but no one ever admitted to loving her before Silas—what with her bulging eyes and the thin layer of hair on her upper lip. Still, Silas brought her love letters and small presents throughout the school year. When he wrapped his mom's diamond earrings for Anita Pelland's Christmas present, she had to set up a meeting with his parents and the principal. "His attentions are innocent," she told us later. "Cute really. I hated to bring everyone into it." After their meeting, Silas still mooned over her, but from afar. On the last day of school, he cried when he said goodbye, though he would continue to see her in town and at school as he always had.

Silas was fifteen when Doug Brickman, the English teacher down at the high school, passed out cameras for a class project. The students brought back what Doug had expected: family shots, pictures of dogs, cats, blurry birds. Silas did too, but his birds weren't blurry—they were detailed and graceful. His dogs leapt in the air, and his cats eyed the lens warily. Doug displayed the students' pictures for the school's open house, but we only noticed Silas's. Even people who didn't have kids in tenth grade stopped to look at his photographs. That night, we began to realize that Silas wasn't odd. He was special.

His parents certainly thought so. They bought him a 35 mm Nikon at the local pawnshop, and from that day on, we never saw him without a camera around his neck. We'd walk outside and see him aiming his lens at our gardens or trees in our yards. He went to the Brickton High School football games and asked to stand on the sidelines to get better shots. From the stands, we watched him in his too-big yellow slicker, which he wore rain or shine. At the beginning of the first quarter, his right pocket bulged with unused canisters of film, but by the end his left pocket was full of used ones. Once, Glenda Edelmeier swore she watched him shoot twenty rolls of film, not including the halftime show.

Doug Brickman watched Silas use two rolls of film shooting people who walked out of the Rite Aid before stopping him. Silas took Doug's parting words to heart: "Take pictures of things that aren't in front of you all the time. Look for something no one else sees."

Silas seemed to consider the advice, because even though he still kept the camera around his neck, none of us saw him take another picture until a couple years ago when he showed up at Anita Pelland's funeral. We didn't think anything of his arrival, as he'd stopped by her classroom everyday until she retired. Besides, she'd taught long division to over half the town. We were all there.

For anyone who'd seen her in the previous year, the viewing was a relief. Instead of wearing diapers and having to be spoon-fed pureed meals, her hair and face were made up, and she was wearing her special occasions dress—the one with the tiny cluster of lilacs twining their way around the navy fabric. It might be wrong to speak ill of the dead, but until everyone saw her dressed up like that, it was as if we'd forgotten who we were supposed to mourn.

Silas walked to the front of the room with his camera out, lens cap swinging. He moved around the casket taking pictures. He stepped close, and we were a little horrified. It's one thing to shoot a football game. It's another to invade the privacy of the dead. When he stepped back to get a wider angle, we waited for Anita's son Samuel to stop him, but he didn't. Silas replaced the lens cap and shook Samuel's hand. There were whispered conversations all over the room.

Two weeks later, Samuel held an open house and invited all of his mom's former students, which, once you added in spouses and children, included most of us. There, we saw what had happened to Silas's pictures. Samuel had one shot blown up, framed, and placed over the mantle, right beside a picture of his father. Somehow, Silas had captured Anita in the best possible way, so that she didn't look like a dead body all made up but like a woman who was proud to look her best, who kept teaching well into her retirement years because she liked children that much. He'd managed to erase the last years of her life, and she looked like the woman we remembered.

After that, it became commonplace to see Silas at all the funerals in town. For a while, some still objected, saying the pictures were blasphemous, but in the end, everyone saw their worth. Eventually, nearly all of us had a picture of a lost loved one framed and placed in a prominent position in the house. When people came to funerals from out of town, they were surprised to see Silas, but we explained that without him, we had no memories. Silas kept our dead alive.

When Harvey Millman drowned in the river and was pulled out bloated and broken, Mr. Masters fixed him up enough for an open casket. At the viewing we could see that Harvey's face was messed up something awful and that it'd taken quite a bit of putty and makeup to mask his injuries. Some said Silas wouldn't be able to use those pictures, but he worked his usual magic and made Harvey look like he would sit up and challenge someone to a game of pickup if we waited just a minute.

It's not that Silas suddenly became normal, but with a camera in his hands, we could overlook his oddities. He still didn't have friends. He ate his lunch alone in the school cafeteria, and he never held a conversation for more than a couple minutes unless it was about photography. Still, we loved him as much as we could. He showed the appropriate respect at funerals and never charged a cent for all his hard work, though we tipped him whenever he brought us pictures of our loved ones—more if we had it, less if we didn't.

Everything changed when Ellen Draper's family moved to town. By then, Silas had begun growing into his looks, and we could see the man he'd become. Apparently, Ellen saw his potential too. Her first day at school, she walked into the cafeteria and placed her lunch tray opposite Silas's. The kids around them watched Ellen say hi, and Silas returned her greeting. They didn't talk much at first, but she sat at his table every day, and pretty soon they were together all the time.

Once she arrived, Silas stopped carrying his camera. Then, he missed a funeral. Janice Evans was the first one who didn't get a funeral picture. Neither did Justin Stephens or Nathan Travers, who died when their cars collided head-on. Or Sara Jane Dawes who was only four and drowned in the creek. But when Silas didn't come to Doug Brickman's funeral, we knew we'd lost him.

During the funerals, Silas and Ellen went to high school basketball games or made out in darkened theaters. They drank pots of coffee at Mom's Place, a diner twenty minutes down the road, and danced too close at the spring formal. Silas talked to the other kids at school and answered questions in his classes. He taught Ellen to drive the stick shift in his old Buick, and she laughed at his corny jokes. He was normal, and we were happy for him, but we missed him. It was a trade-off.

When summer arrived, he and Ellen spent most days at Curtisville Dam, bathing suits on, fishing poles in hand. They joined the sea of teenagers who spent their mornings swimming and catching trout for lunch, turning grassy banks into a beach with transplanted sand and a volleyball court.

Thomas Martin said the Buick made it all the way to the bottom before it hit a walnut tree. He couldn't see what caused the wreck, but he saw the car swerve and disappear over the hill. Thomas held onto branches and dug the sides of his feet into upturned earth to get to the car. Silas stepped out of the driver's side, his nose bloody. When Ellen didn't get out, Thomas expected the worst. He got to the passenger side window, where Ellen sat with her hands resting in her lap, as though she didn't realize what had happened. The windshield was cracked, and a knot had already formed on her forehead. Otherwise, she looked fine.

Still, Thomas drove them to the emergency room. The doctor set Silas's broken nose, diagnosed both of them with concussions, and sent them home with ice packs for their foreheads and directives to wear their seatbelts in the future.

The next morning, Silas went to her house and knocked like he did everyday, but Ellen didn't answer the door. Silas knocked again, and when she still didn't answer, he sat on her porch and waited. None of us saw Ellen in town that day, but we spotted Silas on Ellen's front steps, head in hands, as though trying to figure out what he'd done wrong. When her parents came home from work, he was still there. He stayed on the porch and waited, while they went inside.

A little later, everyone on the block heard the screams that arose from the house. By the time the coroner showed up, we all knew what had happened: Ellen had gone to bed the night before and never woken up. Silas stayed on those steps until late in the night, staring through us all. The coroner, the police, her family—everyone walked around him.

Later, we'd find out that the car accident had caused more than a concussion. The coroner called it a hematoma, said it killed her. None of us wanted to admit it, but our sadness was mixed with glee. Her death was the only thing that would bring Silas back where he belonged, to us.

We all stared when Silas walked into the funeral home. His camera hung over his shoulder, and we watched in silence as he knelt in front of Ellen's casket. Though Mr. Masters had done a good job fixing her up, her forehead still had a lump from smashing into the windshield. Silas leaned forward and kissed her lips, before sitting back and staring at her. We watched the tears drip from the end of his nose onto the velvet top of the kneeler.

Ellen's parents sat at the head of the casket, two chairs set up for them to receive people, but Silas didn't turn to them. Instead, he pulled his camera from his shoulder and put it to his face. He winced when the camera touched his broken nose. We watched him frame his first shot and knew Silas would do something wonderful with Ellen. He stood close enough that only her head would be in the picture, her hair fanned out around her face on that white velvet pillow. Silas clicked the shutter, but before he could frame another, Ellen's father stood and grabbed Silas's shoulder from behind. When he whirled around, Mr. Draper punched Silas's already broken nose. None of us moved, and everyone within ten feet of them later swore they heard Silas's nose break again. Blood poured from both nostrils, wetting his shirt and dripping onto the carpet, but Silas didn't try to staunch the flow. Mr. Draper stood back, his arms at his sides, his chest heaving, as he stared at Silas.

Silas held his gaze. Then, he turned to the crowd, scanned the room, nodded at all of us, and walked down the aisle between the folding chairs and out the front door. Mr. Draper's shoulders sagged, and he went back to sit beside his wife who stared at her hands that lay in her lap. Mr. Draper put his elbows on his knees and leaned his face into the palms of his hands. We continued to hold our breaths, but when the

Drapers didn't move, we gathered our families and headed toward the doors, leaving them alone. Later, Silas's parents told us that Silas hung the picture of Ellen above his bed. They said it was beautiful, his best shot yet.

Weeks later, Silas arrived at Harry James's funeral, camera in hand. A couple of people tried to talk to him, to tell him how much we appreciated his being there, but he ignored us. We sat quietly while he snapped pictures, and the universe was right again.

ABOUT THE AUTHOR

———

Laura Leigh Morris is an assistant professor at Furman University in Greenville, South Carolina, where she teaches creative writing and literature. Before that, she spent three years as the National Endowment for the Arts/Bureau of Prisons Artist-in-Residence at Bryan Federal Prison Camp in Bryan, Texas. She's previously published short fiction in *Appalachian Heritage*, the *Louisville Review*, the *Notre Dame Review*, and other journals. All of her fiction is set in north central West Virginia, where she is originally from and the place she is most at home. From the landscape to the rich variety of people to the long history of resource extraction, the region serves as a rich backdrop to both her life and her stories. *Jaws of Life* is her first book. She is currently hard at work on her first novel. Learn more at lauraleighmorris.com.

CPSIA information can be obtained
at www.ICGtesting.com
Printed in the USA
LVHW01s0717260118
564076LV00004B/4/P